Perhaps She'll Die!

John B Spencer

BLOODLINES

First Published in Great Britain in 1996 by
The Do-Not Press
PO Box 4215
London SE23 2QD

A Paperback Original

ISBN 1 899344 14 4

British Library Cataloguing in Publication Data. A catalogue record for this book is available from the British Library.

Printed and bound in Great Britain by The Guernsey Press Co Ltd.

For Paul and Freddy, not much in common,
except they're both gone.

Chapter 1
I know an old lady,
Who swallowed a cat…

Last night with Giles, the last night before Harry got back from the States, was so good. The best. And, with Giles, it always had been pretty damn good.

Right from the start.

Three weeks ago. Before Celeste had got round to teaching him those special tricks she had picked up from nobody else but Harry. Three weeks. Crash course in keeping Celeste happy. Away from the two bottle a day spiral. Away from climbing up the fucking wall with boredom. Away from missing Harry so much she hated herself for it.

The kid had been willing to learn. Full of himself but still able to ease off, allow Celeste to take the lead. Twenty-seven-years-old, Celeste's age when he was born, starting secondary school when she and Harry had first got together. He hadn't done so bad out of the deal, either.

Celeste smiled.

Saliva, or whatever, coming unglued at the corners of her mouth.

Rolled over in the bed.

Studied his exposed shoulder, the remains of a tan from somewhere hot. Spain? No way, not Giles. Most likely some Greek island nobody else knew about, stuck in the middle of nowhere, the kind of place Harry would never take her because the only food you could get was foreign crap. Celeste touching his back, resenting the elasticity of his skin, his smoothness; did his wife scrub his back for him like she did for Harry? Suddenly angry. Why the fuck should she benefit from all this? From her expertise? She kissed the soft fuzz at the nape of his neck. Giles stirred, turned towards her, buried his face into the cradle between her arm and breast. Not waking. Not yet. Celeste fighting the temptation, savouring the expectation, delaying the moment when, fun-time over, she would have to break the news.

Pity.

But great while it lasted.

Not like all the other dumb fuckheads she seemed to attract, standing there in Harry's bedroom stripped to their fancy patterned jocks, you going *my oh my* like in some old Mae West movie, all the time knowing that what you saw was all you would ever get. No, Giles was different – scrawny little bastard, but full of it once you pressed his button. After that, no complaints. Knew how to tease, too. Tease till you felt like screaming.

Till you did scream.

Full of surprises, Giles.

Like that time, two weeks back, in the hall. Celeste, thrown on her housecoat. come down to say goodbye. Some goodbye! No warning, no by your leave. Right there in the hall, the newspaper boy just five feet away the other side of the front door feeding Harry's *Mail* through the letterbox. Jesus! that had been good.

Celeste couldn't walk through the hall any more without thinking about it. Four days later, bored, pissed, feeling like Harry had been in New York for ever, pressing her shoulders into the banister rail till it hurt, like a brown bear with an itch to scratch…

…found a tree.

But still a kid.

Still only twenty-fucking–seven.

Coming out with dumb shit like: 'I want to explore my sexuality.'

Jesus Christ.

Roll back the years.

Celeste giving him a hard time, pissed off that he was still young enough to be able to say something that stupid. Jealous of his self-obsession, self-importance, like every door that slammed open for him was going to make the world headlines. Sitting up, reaching for the Dunhill cigarettes, the Dunhill lighter.

'Tell me you're joking.'

'What do you mean?'

'Before I wet myself laughing.'

Celeste not exhaling, allowing the smoke to drift out from between her lips, the first warning of fire beneath a hotel room door. She couldn't remember the light being on, but it must have been. Celeste didn't like to smoke in the dark.

Celeste didn't like the dark.

Period.

'Since when did a kid from west London come out with something like, "I want to explore my sexuality?" You got any idea just how dumb that sounds?'

Didn't like the 'kid.'

What kid would?

Of course the light had been on. She could remember his pouty expression. Wanted to hug him for it. Instead, laughed and said, 'Giles, I want to squeeze you until your bones crack.'

Giles playing hard to get.

'Don't tease, Celeste.'

Sulking.

Then: 'Anyway, is that such a bad thing to want to do?'

'You're asking me?'

Blowing smoke in his face.

'You know I hate that.'

The cigarette glowing between her fingers. Giles, early on, saying: 'You know it's the slipstream that's most dangerous.' Celeste: 'That's why I smoke, dope.' Give him a few weeks – only she wouldn't be – Giles would be suggesting, then demanding, that she didn't smoke in bed. Thank Christ it wasn't going to last that long. 'Hold this a minute, would you?' Celeste had said, passing him the cigarette. Then she was beneath the quilt, her mouth searching out the warm funk of her own juice on his body…

Like the spray of a cat. Defining territory.

Not her territory.

Cuckoo in the nest.

Saying: 'What would your wife think, the smell of another woman?'

Licking him clean.

Hearing *him* scream.

That had been the first night in her bed. Harry's bed…

…And, he still hadn't asked her the usual dumb question.

The first time, the really first time, had been three nights before. Press preview, new film by that old goat, Max Duncan – Christ! Celeste couldn't stand the sight of him – made porno movies, black and white junk, young street-cred journalists all of a sudden conjuring up crap like 'Erotica As Art On A Shoestring'. Porno movies backed by Harry's money. Harry laughing, that was rare, but, showing her those clippings just before he flew off to New York, he cracked up. Come the night, Harry still three thousand five hundred miles away, invite still stuck there on the mantlepiece, she thought, 'Why the fuck not?' Up till then, Celeste had thought ICA was something to do with soap powder.

'So, what did you think?'

Giles talking to her across the rim of a wine glass.

Celeste's first impression:

Thinking, not saying…

Shouldn't you be home finishing off some homework?

Christ! They let them out of school early these days.

Not even interested, but then, wanting to make a point to the adolescent bitch with the crew cut and ankle boots. Let her know, one woman to another, that competition was more than just a big mouth and a *You can fuck me if you're lucky* attitude.

Let her know that being sweet nineteen wasn't necessarily all it took.

Giles was parked in a slip road off The Mall. Dark shadow of the back of the Pall Mall Club building rising high to the right. Trees whispering. Lamps throwing pools of orange light, turning leaves and grass grey. The car was a slate green Morris Minor, would have fitted in the boot of Harry's Roller with room to spare.

'This is a car?'

'Vintage fifty-eight. Classic small family saloon. Run for ever just so long as you check the steering pinions on a regular basis.'

'You lost me, Giles.'

'Basic design fault. Front wheel collapses, you cartwheel down the motorway.' Boyish grin. 'You either love them or you hate them.'

Celeste, 'Read my lips.'

Giles had to push forward the front seat so they could climb into the back. facing up The Mall. the roundabout and the lights of Buckingham Palace ahead of them.

'What happens if the Queen comes out, decides to take the corgis for a walk?'

'Won't she be surprised?'

'You don't want to go somewhere?'

'We are somewhere.'

'I mean…'

'You mean, I don't seem the type.'

'I mean, I'm easy if you are.'

'Try me.'

There on the back seat, the warm surprise as he entered her, that moment always a surprise, the gasp she could never help, forced between clenched teeth, Celeste's knee painful against the metal ashtray, palms flat against the roof of the car, pushing hard. Just like the first time, ever? You were supposed to always remember the first time ever. Celeste didn't. Wondering why she didn't. Coming down, now. 'Erotica As Art On A Shoestring' – too fucking right!

Lighting a cigarette.

Giles didn't complain that first time.

'You didn't call out your wife's name. Things can't be that great on the home front.'

'How did you know I was married?'

'You must be joking.'

Adjusting themselves.

The dampness growing cold.

'I'd have called out yours, only I don't know it.'

'Smooth-talking bastard.'

Remembering Harry singing, to the tune of *All of Me*, Christ, Harry had a lousy voice. 'I took the best, I took Celeste…' Using it.

'In case there's a next time, it's Celeste. Rhymes with The Best.'

'You better give me your number.'

'No, you give me your number, your work number.'

And there had been plenty of times over those next three weeks, Harry away in New York. Now today, this morning, Harry was coming home, Ross already on his way to Gatwick to pick him up, and there was time for one last time. Watching Giles, still asleep, thinking how last night he had disappointed her, nearly ruined it, finally got round to asking the usual dumb question they always got round to asking…

'What is it your old man does to afford all this?'

All this.

The house that Harry built.

Remembering the exact date, a Tuesday. Tuesday, eighteenth of December, seven years back. She and Harry had been Christmas shopping in Knightsbridge and Harry had suggested an early supper at Mr Chow's. Celeste trying to make sense of the menu: 'Crab Butterfly? What the fuck is a Crab Butterfly?' Trying to picture the combination of a crab and a butterfly, any combination, that would make any sense. 'Harry, couldn't we just get a takeaway?' Harry taking the letter from his wallet, neatly folded, passing it across the table to her. Noticing, first, the embossed letterhead, *Sackville Rose, South Audley Street, Mayfair*. Harry saying, 'Happy Christmas,' big oafish smile on his face. Harry liked to spring surprises. Good or bad. Celeste still had the estate agent's spec-sheet, kept it in a bottom drawer along with a pile of other junk.

She could remember how it read.

The exact wording.

Like a fairy tale…

Detached luxury family home overlooking Hampstead Heath. MUST be seen to be fully appreciated. Master bedroom with en suite bathroom and jacuzzi, five additional bedrooms with en suite shower/WC, two luxury bathrooms, exercise room with sunbed and sauna, through lounge with mezzanine floor – Celeste had wondered about that until she discovered that mezzanine meant a couple of steps that you always tripped over on the way back from the bar to the sofa – *rumpus room, fully equipped fitted kitchen, library* – library! for fuck's sake – *conservatory, reception/cloakroom, utility/boiler-room, approx. half acre of well tended gardens front and rear, lawn and gazebo.*

'Gazebo! We going to have wild animals running around, Harry?'

'It's a summer house, Celeste.'

'Joke, Harry. You think I don't know what a gazebo is?'

Harry worried that he might have offended. Spoilt the surprise. Celeste reaching across and touching his hand, wanting to say, had wanted to say ever since, that that cold December night, with the sleet coming down and the traffic piling up along the Brompton Road, cars misting up, wipers going, fog lights on, it had seemed like the most beautiful poem she had ever read. But still she said: 'What is all this, Harry? Family home? We don't have a family. What is it you think we are going to do with all these rooms?'

'Whatever, doll, that's up to you.' Harry had said. 'I signed the paperwork this morning.'

Celeste knew when Harry wasn't listening because he always missed the point. When Harry was listening. he never, ever, missed the point.

'That's an awful lot of bathrooms for two people, Harry.'

'It's what makes you special. Celeste,' Harry said, 'You're not easily satisfied.'

Hampstead Lane.

Overlooking the Heath. Overlooking the whole of London. On a clear day you could see Shooters Hill, Blackheath. Watch the passenger jets, all in a line, following the Thames into Heathrow... Concorde, four-twenty-five every afternoon, you could set your watch by it. Two hundred and five thousand pounds, in 1977, you have to remember... How the fuck did Harry get his hands on that kind of money?

What is it your old man does to afford all this?

The usual dumb question.

'He brokers deals. Puts people who need money in touch with people who have money. The deal comes off, Harry takes a cut.'

Vague in her answer. The way Harry was vague whenever she asked him the same question. Before she gave up asking.

'Pinstripe and bowler?'

'Where have you been, Giles?'

There were no photographs of Harry around the place. Harry didn't like having his picture taken. Not like those dumb bastards who had a wall full of pictures of themselves with this celebrity, that celebrity, glasses in their hands, eyes glazed and shiny, pissed out of their heads.

'Is that it?'

'Is that what?'

'I mean, they must be some kind of deals, he can afford all this.'

All this.

The same dumb fucking question.

Draw the kid a picture.

No: join some of the dots for him.

'He owns clubs.'

'Clubs? What kind of clubs?'

'Drinking clubs... gambling joints.'

Feed the kid a little of what Harry was really about.

'The Columbine Club, you ever heard of it?'

'He owns the Columbine Club?'

'Last I heard.'

And not believing a word of it...

Before she gave up asking.

About the time Harry bought his first Roller, like a big kid... Corniche. He'd given her a pillarbox red 911, but she traded it in for a white Mercedes 281 Sports after six months. The Porsche, not her kind of car, didn't like the sound the engine made, like a clockwork motor, you had to wind a key. This was six months after Tim died, long before she had got used to the fact of him being dead. Still wasn't used to it. What a fucking *stupid* thing to happen. Harry and Tim, they went back all the way. Blood brothers. Partners in everything except her. Tim had never made a move in that direction – not once.

Unlike some of Harry's so-called friends.

'Is that it?'

Sat there in Harry's bed.

Harry's wife not enough for him.

Wanting his whole fucking history, too.

Hearing herself talking just like Harry: 'So how much do you want?'

Hating herself for talking like Harry. Wanting Giles to shut up, grab his clothes, fuck off out of Harry's house. Thought of telling him to do just that, only it was one-thirty in the morning. If Giles left now, forget sleep... not without the diazepam, a few G&Ts, Harry's fucking video library downstairs in the lounge, so much empty space around her, she would have to keep all the lights on.

Saying, 'He funds films – that Max Duncan shit, you love so much.'

'He financed that?'

'Among others.'

'So that's how come you were at the ICA?'

'Is that so strange?'

'Since you ask, yes.'

Giles had his arms folded behind his head, skinny torso, stretching. Harry was so big, opulent, musky...

So different.

'Some guys, they make it look easy, making money.'

'Nothing comes easy, honey.'

'Like the whole wide world was just sat there waiting to get ripped off.'

'You got it in one.'

He was just a kid.

How could you stay angry with a kid?

'Access,' Giles said, 'That's the buzz word right now.'

'You got that, honey, any time you want.'

Only it wasn't true.

Not any more.

She stroked his chest, found a nipple, squeezed hard to wake him. Most men liked that, but not so many were willing to admit it. Giles stirred, ready for her. 'What's the hurry, lover?' Celeste said, her finger pushing hard into his crevice as he entered her.

One last time.

Before she broke the news.

Harry was coming home.

Ross McManaman didn't like airports.

Especially, didn't like Gatwick.

Glitzy shopping mall on the first floor, Gatwick Village? Who the fuck did they think they were kidding? Powdered tea in a plastic cup, UHT milk, one of those little containers, the milk always went over your suit, you tried to open it. Full breakfast, you must be joking, not at those prices.

The place packed with families, booked their package holiday somewhen in the last century, wandering around like lost fucking sheep, blocking gangways, the kids screaming, the old lady carrying on about the back-packers sleeping across three seats, never thinking to do anything about it… wake them up, tell them to shift their fucking arses.

Jesus–H–Christ!

Pathetic.

Ross dumping his tea into a litter bin – could do with empty-ing – checked his watch, took the express walkway through to the arrivals lounge. The overhead monitors still reading: *New York Flight TWA l338: Delayed Due To Weather Conditions. ETA*

9.45 – just like they had since eight-thirty. Ross standing back from the divider rail, distancing himself from the waiting crowd, watching the doors to the Customs Hall, beyond the divider, tourists coming through, then the stragglers. Wondering what it was about the stragglers had caught the attention of the Customs, got them stopped going through the green channel, baggage searched.

Remembering his brother-in-law, Colm, his wife Mary's youngest brother, surprised the whole family when he went into Customs & Excise, the stories he used to tell them before warehouse-bonded bourbon and Budweiser chaser put him in an early grave, six years last Christmas. The Stuffer's and Swallowers' Room, where they put you till you couldn't help but crap. The way the innocent always looked as guilty as the guilty while their bags were being searched and the guilty stayed looking guilty. Dead give-aways, like the guy with the red luggage transfer tags – he was such a seasoned traveller, how come he was looking nervous? Colm's story about the classy looking woman, walks bold as brass through the green channel, straight up to the bar and orders a large brandy. When they searched her, found she was carrying cocaine worth half a million, street level – fucking amazing how people thought it was some kind of game, how, if you cleared the Customs channels, you were home and dry. Ross pointing this out to Harry once, coming back from France through Dover, the bloke in the car park, lounging against a Transit, looked like a dock worker taking a break... clocking the cars as they left the port area. Harry and Ross laughing at the thought of some poor schmucks, slapping each other on the back, breaking out the champagne to celebrate, the bloke calling for back-up, flagging them down...

Ross, now, playing a game, passing the time. Deciding who he would have pulled – bearded kid coming through on his own, quilted anorak, sneakers, too fucking obvious, looked like a mule, for christ's sake! Ross had been strip-searched, once, rubber gloves, the works. Flight into Heathrow from Riyadh, connecting at Düsseldorf. He ever caught one of those bastards out of uniform. The Customs Hall throwing up again. Straw hats, Bermudas, duty-free bags spilling cartons of Marlborough Lights, some of them searching the crowd for familiar faces. Big grins, hugs, kisses, after two weeks in Torremolinos...?

Girl with a sailboard, strapped sideways on to her baggage trolley, held with spider-clips, looking out across the arrivals lounge, sussing, no way was she going to make it through that crowd. Group of men where the divider rails funnelled to a narrow exit channel, all knew each other, some in liveried uniform, holding placards – *Mr Grey, Westlake Constructions, Mars, Clearform, Toshiba, Ralph* – all the names written in biro or felt-tip. Ross thinking, How come handwritten? They could afford to lay on a fucking chauffeur.

Which reminded Ross…

One big reason he hated hanging around at airports.

Reminded him that most of the time he was nothing but Harry's fucking chauffeur.

Next time Ross glanced at the overhead monitors he didn't register the change. Had been checking the screens so many times he wasn't even reading them any more. Had to watch the whole sequence through again. *New York Flight TWA1338: Landed.*

Landed…

Harry was down.

Ross turned and began walking towards the exit that led to the short-term car park. A kid grabbed his arm. Jeans, trainers, American accent, from out of nowhere in the crowd.

'Hey, mister, maybe you can help me.'

Keeping pace with Ross, sideways on, skipping from foot to foot, keeping eye contact all the way: 'Some guy grabbed my wallet. Cash, cards, everything. If I can get into London, meet up with my buddy, I'll be okay…'

Then: 'You think you can let me have some money, buy a ticket?'

Ross shaking his arm free, still walking.

The kid saying, 'If I made it worth your while?'

Ross stopping.

Turning to face the kid.

Nervous eyes, showing too much white. Pale… blind boil on his chin, visible through the light beard.

The kid saying, 'What do you say?'

Poxy little fucker!

'User, yeah?'

'Huh.'

'You heard me, kid.'

Ross seeing it in the kid's eyes, wondering whether he should get out of there, evaporate back into the crowd, the kid thinking, Where does this guy get off, coming at me like this? The kid saying, 'Maybe, once in a while, you know how it goes. Nothing I can't handle.'

Ross staring at the kid.

'No bullshit, man. What I told you about losing my wallet, meeting my buddy, that was straight.'

Ross looked above the kid's head at the main arrivals display board. Found *TWA1338*. *Landed* had been replaced with *In Customs Hall*. One thing about Harry's flight being delayed, they would miss the worst of the morning traffic heading back into town...

'Get lost, kid,' he said.

This time she was going to murder Giles, really kill him, with her own two bare hands.

Denise ran the brush through Mandy's tangled hair, counting the strokes. Six years old. Hardly believable. She had lived with Giles, put up with Giles, for all of six years. Stroking away her anger. 'When will it be tomorrow?' Mandy had asked, when she was three. Time went so quickly – yesterday, it seemed like to Denise. A car horn sounded from the road outside. Denise glanced at the electric wall clock. *Running slow. must get a new battery*. 'Do your coat up properly, Mandy. It's cold.' She did it herself as she was speaking. Mandy's smart new school blazer. 'Have you got your note for Miss Watson? Good. Hurry, don't keep Jane waiting.'

At the front door she kissed Mandy on the lips, turned her, propel led her forward, waved to Jane waiting in the Renault 4L with her daughter, Kate. in the back seat. 'Be good, darling,' she shouted after Mandy.

Mandy.

Conceived and born in Denise's eighteenth year. Alive today, existing, only because her future mother had felt silly saying no to her future father. Silly. Drunk on too much white wine and that sickly blue cocktail they had all sipped through straws from the same glass in that bar that Ernest Hemingway used to drink in. Then that horrible hotel room near the Gard du Nord, alone with Giles after Barbara had paired off with... she couldn't remember his name. Self-assured. Much better looking than Giles. They had been to the Rodin Museum that afternoon, figures naked and carved in stone or cast in bronze. The cathedral-like atmosphere. The celebration of the human form... The Eternal Idol, The Metamorphosis of Ovid. It hadn't been at all like that with Giles. She had thought she would feel so adult, so bohemian, there in a Paris hotel room with her first lover. Instead, she had thrown up in the washbasin. Giles, from the bed, making a joke of it. 'Don't worry,' he had said. 'I always have that effect on girls.'

Did he *still* have that effect on girls?

Two years later they had seen The Kiss at the Tate Gallery. Four years ago they were still able to laugh about it. 'Look, Mandy,' Giles had said, holding his daughter up, 'There's your Mummy and Daddy.'

The bastard!

Why didn't he ring her, at least?

Despite herself, she still worried. There *might* have been an accident. It was ten to nine. She waved once more as Jane's Renault turned the corner at the end of the avenue. The last leaves had fallen from the poplars. The strong wind last night. How long would it take the council to clear them up this year? What time *did* she get to sleep last night? Giles usually got to the Magazine around ten-thirty. He would ring her then... like he always did.

She picked up the milk from the doorstep, went inside. Made filter coffee with hot milk. Warmed a croissant, even though she wasn't hungry. Sat at the kitchen table. Giles had said, that first time he had admitted to sleeping with somebody else, eighteen months after they were married. Mandy was two: 'It's when I don't come home at night, you need to start worrying.' She was worried, but why? What would his excuse be this time. Another grant misappropriation scandal, moonlighting to meet the deadline? Another drinking session with Chris, his editor, Chris needing a sympathetic ear, some buddy-buddy advice on his own marriage problems? Seven nights in the last three weeks. Seven bloody nights! Even Giles was going to run out of excuses at this rate.

The phone rang.

It was too early. Perhaps something really had happened. Denise reached up and lifted the receiver from the wall mounting. It was Jane.

'It's only me. Just to say they made it okay.'

Only me.

Every morning at nine-fifteen Jane rang just to say they had made it okay. Why should she have assumed it would be anything to do with Giles? Of course, there were times when she had every reason to worry. Like when Giles went out on one of those 'field investigations' with a cassette recorder and microphone strapped to him, hidden under his clothing. But Giles always let her know when he was doing anything like that, boastful, thought it was glamorous.

Glamorous?

Rather sordid, Denise always thought.

'Kate has the sniffles. I think she might be going down with something. Do hope she doesn't pass it on to your Mandy. It's such a bind having a sick child to look after, what with everything else.'

'Well, at least it keeps them quiet.'

'Yes, there is that, I suppose. Anyway… coffee, usual time?'

Usual time.

When Jane dropped Mandy off from school at four o'clock.

Of course, it was very nice of her to give Mandy a lift every day but Denise sometimes thought that the price was too high. Dinner not started, Mandy and Kate creating havoc in the living room just after she'd tidied up – it was all right for Jane, she had that Dutch girl, Onya, back home looking after their little Terry, preparing the evening meal, keeping the place shipshape while she sat around drinking endless cups of coffee, discussing the pros and cons of sending Kate to the French Lysee next year.

'I don't mind admitting it would be a stretch, no second holidays abroad for a little while; but, when it's a matter of one's child's education, one must be prepared to make sacrifices, don't you think?'

Denise agreeing. And if, as sometimes happened, they had a glass of wine to wash down the coffee, just a tipple, as Jane would put it? What was it Jane had come out with that afternoon, after they had got through a whole bottle of Rioja between them, after Jane was through with her impromptu

Spanish lesson, how the 'j' is always pronounced as a 'k', explaining how the number stamped on the reverse of the bottle indicated the quality of the wine, which pressing, though she could never remember – high-pitched laugh – whether it was one or eight was the superior wine – oh, yes! That was it. Her and Peter's sex life. How she loved to get on to that subject. And how Denise hated it. 'He does look such a rather dry old stick, you'd hardly believe it of him, would you?' Denise longing to shock her into silence, tell her Giles liked to chop chilli pepper then masturbate…

Though where on earth she had got that image from.

Because it wasn't true.

At least, she thought it wasn't true.

Jane still wittering on on the other end of the line.

'Actually, Jane,. would you mind terribly?'

'Well, of course, darling, if it's inconvenient.'

Pause.

Then:

'You and Giles, everything is all right between you two, isn't it?'

'Whatever gave you that impression?'

'Oh, you know me. Just take no notice. It's just you do seem a little distracted just lately, I was wondering if there was anything the matter. You can always talk to me, you know that, don't you, Denise.'

Whatever gave you that impression.

Said too quickly.

Defensively.

Jane wouldn't have missed that, nosy bloody bitch. Her and Peter the perfect couple. She could have told Jane a thing or two about her precious Peter. Their pre-Christmas drinks party last year, Denise trapped between little Terry's highchair and the washing machine, Peter spilling red wine down his white Aran jumper: 'I've never been able to say this before… I've never felt like this before. Why don't we give it a go, Denise, see where it leads us?' Denise laughing, 'Peter, you're as drunk as a lord!' Thinking, are all men like this? Is Giles really any different? Any more reprehensible?

'It's just I've got the council surveyor coming over at three-thirty.'

'And about time, too. You know there's not the money available there used to be…' Roofing, loft insulation, guttering, window frames, re-pointing, levelling of ground floor joists, the complete history of Jane and Peter's four bedroom Nash-designed semi on Mayberry Crescent, how could Denise have been so stupid as to bring up the subject?

Finally, '…Anyway, darling, I'll just drop Mandy off at the usual time and be on my way.'

Usual time.

Was there anything Jane didn't always do at the usual time.

Surprised to find herself smiling… well, according to what Jane told her about her and Peter, yes there was.

Giles had said, once, 'Why do we always wait till we are in bed? It's so predictable, gets to be like brushing your teeth every night. We didn't used to be like that.'

'That's only because we didn't used to have a bed to go to.'

Giles's parents' house in Kew, living room floor, the television blaring out from the back room beyond the closed sliding wooden dividers. Is that why Giles's parents had the television on so loud? Because they knew? Denise had been sharing a bed-sit with three other girls, one of them Barbara, in Elgin Crescent, off Ladbroke Grove. There had never been any privacy there. Before Mandy began to show. Before they decided against an abortion, told their parents, got married.

'I'd feel silly doing it over the kitchen table.' Always that word… silly. 'Besides, Mandy might come down, she isn't asleep, yet.'

Giles patronising: 'It's taken four years to persuade you that it can be more fun with the light on. I suppose I'll just have to be patient.'

But, it wasn't more fun. Not with Giles staring at her like that – 'Don't close your eyes!' feeling like she was in some pornographic film.

Was it her fault she felt like that?

All her fault.

That one time she had been unfaithful to Giles. He was in Brighton for the week, covering the convention. She had taken Mandy on the train to stay with Barbara who was living in Wales, now, near Aberystwyth, working as a freelance illustrator. On the Friday night there had been a party, somebody's birthday party, and towards the end, seeing the way things were developing, Barbara had offered to baby-sit. That *had* been fun. Denise had surprised herself, wondering later how much of it had been a desire to impress Barbara, show her that she was, after all, still a free spirit…

Or had it been more to do with the local grass they all grew?

Hardly fair on Jack.

He had charmed the pants off her. Quite literally.

Smiling to herself at the awfulness of the joke…

Big old wooden bathtub on the kitchen floor. Flagstones, icy cold on bare feet. Hot water, in buckets, from the boiler. Later, upstairs in bed, doing all those things Giles always wanted her to do, feeling good, wanted – not used. Was it because Giles asked her that she couldn't, not with him? Was that why, afterwards, she had felt so guilty…

…because she hadn't closed her eyes?

Felt like *that*.

Silly.

Jack always rang whenever he was in London. They had been to lunch together, twice. Denise had refused him on both occasions. Jack had said he wasn't going to give up on her.

Denise hoped not.

'Jane, you're a peach,'

'Later, darling, bye-ee!'

'Bye, Jane.'

It was nine-thirty. Another hour before Giles would ring. She heard *The Guardian* being pushed through the letterbox.

Or was it more of those bloody circulars?

What Harry loved most about the Roller was the mascot. Cute little serving maid, skirts thrown up, bending forward ready to take it from behind, on the run, no messin', wham, bam, thank you, mam.

Running with the fantasy.

Hearing the 'Oouch' as he put it in to her.

'How' without the 'h', but with the 'ch'.

A surprised, 'Sir!!!?'

Chrome goddess.

Harry was tired. Too many scotches on the flight. Focusing on the mascot perched there on the cliff-edge of the bonnet.

Knowing he loved that girl. Loved her as much as he loved Celeste. Why not? They were two of a kind. How the fuck could anybody concentrate on driving once you had *that* image fixed in your head?

Only, today, Harry wasn't driving. No way. A23 into Central London, a fucking joke. Ross in one of his moods.

'That time of the month is it, again, Ross?' he'd said to him when he clocked his face, waiting there in the arrivals lounge.

'I've been stuck here since eight-thirty, Harry.'

'You should be so lucky. Here, make yourself useful, grab this bag, will you?'

Stuck here since eight-thirty. Harry, meanwhile, making it straight from Nestor's club on the South Side, no sleep, to the airport, then stuck at Kennedy waiting for the fog to lift – what the fuck did they have instruments for? Then, when they did get up there, the captain's announcement, like some big kid, turbulence is expected… *'Please fasten seat belts and extinguish all cigarettes.'* A thousand foot drop in the time it took to spill your drink. Almost a screamer. Harry not sure if he had screamed or not. First fucking class all the way – only, first class didn't get you there any quicker, and it didn't guarantee you a place on the life raft after your 747 fell through forty-five thousand feet of thin air into the mid-Atlantic. Life rafts? Who the fuck did they think they were kidding? And then Ross standing there with his long face on, Harry saying to him, 'That time of month, is it, Ross?' Well, fuck Ross, and his being there since eight-thirty.

Next time, he would fly Concorde.

Charter his own plane.

Buy his own plane…

If this deal with the greasers came off.

Finally, had enough of Ross's moody – it was true what they said, all you could hear was the clock – saying, 'It's like, in the States, they have a completely different attitude. No fucking about. Everybody knows exactly what they're in it for, and making no bones about it.'

Stuck in the mid-morning traffic at Kennington Oval. The curved stretch running round the west side of the cricket ground. Jesus! London was such a scum-hole. What were all these fuckers doing on the road, anyway? Didn't any of them have offices to go to? Ross, strumming his fingers on the wheel, his eyes following a black girl high-strutting down the pavement, nice pair of pins, short skirt, three-quarter fake fur bought in some Oxfam Shop. A sixth sense telling her she was being watched, looking towards the Roller.

Harry saying to Ross, knowing it would annoy him: 'Fancy giving it one, then?' Then: 'Nice little pointed titties. Could poke your eye out with one of them, she could.'

The girl, over her shoulder, smiling without breaking stride.

'Ross, I do believe you've scored.'

'Do me a favour, Harry.'

The girl fighting the temptation to look back one more time.

'Godiver she does.'

She did.

'What'd I tell you, Ross?'

'Sometimes, you're like a big fuckin' kid, Harry.'

The Roller wasn't a set of wheels you could ignore. There were drivers who gave way out of deference, others who made a point of cutting you up. People were always looking in the window to see if they recognised anybody famous. Leave it on the road overnight, some bastard always felt obliged to carve his initials in the paintwork with a door key.

Rollers, you just couldn't ignore. Especially Harry's Roller. One-off job. Custom built originally for Douglas Fairbanks Jnr who, for weird reasons of his own, wanted it to look like a '57 Chevrolet. White coachwork, chrome fairing, cream leather interior, whitewall tyres, the lot. Mulliners must have done their nut when they got the specification. Harry had bought it from a rock star, drummer in a major league sixties band who used to travel the world trashing hotel rooms. When Harry had gone down to the drummer's mansion in Ardingly, near the coast at Littlehampton, to take possession, there had been a scrap of paper tucked under the wipers on the windscreen that read: *Tax in the Post*. Harry had liked that. A fifty-five grand limousine and a scrap of paper on the windscreen read: *Tax in the Post*.

Harry's friends thought he was crazy when they saw it. So what was wrong with this year's model. Harry could afford it. Apart from the radiator it didn't even look like a Roller, for fuck's sake, what was the point? 'Just so long as it fuckin' drives like one,' Harry had said. And, of course, there was the gorgeous little chrome prick-tease perched there at the end of the bonnet.

Harry thought: Perhaps Ross is right, perhaps I am like a big fucking kid, said: 'Bertram, did he sort The Brewer like I told him?'

'Too soddin' right, he did, greedy little bastard.'

'Who's been a silly boy then, eh, Ross?'

'What'd you want me to do about him?'

'I'll sleep on it.'

The builder's Transit in front found first gear. Lengths of two-by-four protruding between the doors, doors held tight against the wood by a loop of orange nylon rope wound through the handles. Big dark four-storey building on the left, a school. Kids in blue uniforms hanging around in groups, staking out their territory, smacking heads, the smaller kids kicking footballs around. Another world. Sliding from view as the traffic crawled forward.

Another world.

The whole of fucking London was another world!

'Yanks, they don't return your call, it's because they remember they don't want to talk to you. Over here, it's because they forgot you called.'

'Least, here, you don't get all the bullshit, Harry.'

'Is that what you think, Ross?'

They were on Vauxhall Bridge, traffic thinner, the river looking cold and dirty, Harry thinking how his old man used to swim in that when he was a kid. Ross putting his foot down, staying level with a Ford Fiesta busting a gut to overtake them on the inside, matching acceleration, waiting till the driver of the Fiesta hit the brake first as they approached the red on the far side of the bridge, on the junction with the Embankment.

Harry was thrown forward against his seat-belt.

Smiled at Ross.

'So, now, who's the big fuckin' kid?'

Looked across at the driver of the Fiesta, staring straight ahead, left arm posed across the passenger seat, winding the revs, willing the lights to change, get away from these crazy fuckers.

Fifteen hundred ccs.

A clown.

When the amber showed, Ross let him go.

'Tingo Maria?' he said to Harry.

'They came to us, what more can you expect?'

'Reasonable?'

'As it happens, a right fuckin' gymkhana.'

Vauxhall Bridge Road. Victoria Station. Black cabs, red dou-
ble-deckers, traffic solid everywhere you looked.

'So? Is it sorted?'

'Put it this was – Tingo Maria's a long way from New York
City.' There had to be interest, didn't there?'

Grosvenor Place. On their right, the long high unbroken
wall surrounding the grounds of Buckingham Palace. Some
back garden. Now that was *real* money.

'You tell me, Harry.'

Hyde Park Corner.

'Do me a favour,' Harry said. 'Just drive, will you?'

Smiling to himself.

Knowing what Ross was thinking.

Knowing he was thinking…

Nothing but Harry's fucking chauffeur.

After a while, he said:

'So, tell me about Celeste.'

'I don't believe you!'

Emphasis on the *you*. Meaning, I don't believe somebody
like you could actually exist, not, I don't believe what
you've just now told me. Only, on reflection, Giles realising that
he probably had meant it that way as well.

How could she possibly?

Treating him like a glorified one-night-stand.

'Just like that?' he added.

Celeste reading it all.

Amused.

'There's no easy way to say it, honey. You're a big boy
now…' – but was he really? – '…you can take it.'

Celeste still in bed, Giles at a psychological disadvantage,
half-dressed, socks, pants, pulling on his Pepé jeans, upper
torso still bare. Why *did* men always look ridiculous when they
were dressing? Harry often walked around the house in just his
woollen socks. Black ones. One hundred per cent pure wool.
Complaining about the decorative floor tiles: 'Fuck knows why

I let you talk me into them. Like walking on ice,' he said, 'the fortune I spend on central heating.'

Harry could be mean where it didn't count.

Generous, where it counted.

'I'll call you in a couple of days, we can meet up for a drink, talk it over.'

'There's nothing to talk over, Giles.'

T-shirt. Denim shirt with studs. Snapping the cuffs.

'Harry, does he work regular hours? Maybe, I could come over one afternoon.'

Still not getting the point.

Christ, how Celeste hated it when he voiced Harry's name.

Searched for the word.

Impertinence?

No, two words…

Fucking liberty.

Why didn't he just sod off right now. It was eight-thirty. Harry's plane would be down by now, Ross there waiting to drive him back. There were no cigarettes left in the pack on the bedside table. Celeste threw back the quilt and got up, allowing Giles a full view of what was no longer his to have. Rubbing it in. Hoping he was going to get the point, and soon. Celeste was proud of her body. Often wondered how it would have worked out if she and Harry had had children. There were plenty of women her age at the health club who were mothers… who still looked pretty good. You just had to look after yourself, that was all. But it was too late to start thinking about all that now. What was it they had called her at the clinic?

Aging primate.

She had wanted to kick the doctor's teeth down the back of his throat. Given the chance, he wouldn't have said no, snotty little bastard!

Come over one afternoon?

'I don't think that would be a very good idea.' Celeste was rummaging in her handbag for another pack of Dunhills, couldn't find any, threw the bag on to the bed in exasperation.

Jesus!

Giles, dressed now, was searching his jacket pocket for his car keys. An automatic habit. Just as soon as the jacket went on. Nervous, out of place, him dressed, her naked, as if none of this had ever happened.

Finally getting the point.

'What would Harry do if he ever found out? Would he divorce you?'

Celeste had to laugh at that one.

'He's not going to find out.'

'Is he the jealous type? Would he want to take a swing at me?'

At me...

Celeste noticed.

Not concerned that Harry might want to do anything to her.

She found a long stub in the ashtray, straightened it out, found her lighter.

Said:

'Harry ever took a swing at you, you'd be dead.'

Chapter 2
Fancy that…
<u>*To swallow a cat.*</u>

Hammersmith Broadway…
Traffic still tailed back in every direction, but no problem for the bike. North on to Shepherds Bush Road, past the nick, pull in to top up the tank. Last fiver till fuck knows when, handing it across to the old geezer behind the pay desk, half inch a Mars Bar while he's making a big thing of studying the note, holding it up to the light, no fucking idea what he should be looking for… geriatric old sod should treat himself to some new glasses… pushover, this place would be… just nip out back to the bike for the hammer…

No way!

Wrong time of day.

Too busy. Some hero done karate one night a week for the last couple of months might walk in, and what with the filth just down the road.

Worth bearing in mind, though.

Distinct possibilities.

Back out on to Shepherds Bush Road, left at Bush Green, dossers lying all over the grass like some nutter had sprayed the green with an Uzi Automatic, dead to the world, poor fuckers. Goldhawk Road, heading west, the bike purring like a dream. Cookie's eel pie and mash shop on the corner by the market. Ray's old man could remember Cookie's being there from when he was a kid, even – and that was going back some. Double-decker pulling out from the bus garage just before the bridge. Oblivious bastard! Ray dropping down one, opening the throttle, lovely ratio the CBR 600, weaving around the bus, the driver sounding his horn, Ford Granada coming the other way, braking, but he didn't have to, Ray clocking the driver's expression as he was through the gap, grey suit jacket on a hanger in the back…

Fucking rep.

Fucking red too...

Teasing the throttle at the lights, winding the revs till he could hear the air induction kicking in, waiting on the green. Geezers clocking the machine, red and black streamlined fairing, evil great fucking mosquito sat there on the road. Posse of dreads outside the Liquormart across the road, steel shutters still down – just like in the films, in New York – having a laugh about something or other. Posey bastards, who the fuck did they think they were? Off their fucking heads most of the time on their ganja...

Cans of brew.

Thunderbird.

Ray thought about the hammer again. Thought about pulling over to the curb, getting it out of the pannier, crossing the road...

Breaking a few heads.

Wondered what Susanne would think, him doing something like that. Her reading about it in the local papers. All his mates reading about it in the local papers. He'd be a hero. Well worth the aggravation, whatever the filth threw at him, though he doubted they'd come down too heavy. The filth didn't like those black bastards any more than he did. Probably give him a medal. Susanne could cut out the picture from the front page, have it framed, him standing there with the hammer, big fifteen-pounder, steel handle, leather grip, British made...

It took a fifteen-pounder to take out a Chubb.

Did Susanne know that?

Not very likely.

'You're a shy one, aren't you?'

That was the first thing she ever said to him. Out at that party in Northolt. Some bird's parents away for the fortnight. State they left the place. Stupid bitch whose party it was in hysterics... what did she expect?

Ray away on the amber.

Holding first.

Show those bastards.

Eighteen months back, was it? Couldn't have been *that* long. Have to asked Susanne, she'd know, she was good at remembering that sort of thing.

He'd been looking at her all evening, couldn't take his eyes off her, wearing one of those baggy off-one-shoulder T-shirts, white bra strap showing, kept slipping off her shoulder while she was dancing with her mate. *Wild Boys*, Duran Duran, it was – what would you expect in Northolt? Good sound system, though. All separates, Moranz speakers, must have cost a few bob, that lot. Finally, she's come over to him, spoken first, head about level with his chest. He hadn't realised she was so short. 'You're a shy one, aren't you.' That's what she said. Ray thought she was taking the piss, having a laugh with her mates, smiling at him like that.

Like she fancied him.

'What gives you that idea?'

'You've been staring at me all night, why didn't you come over, ask me for a dance?'

'I don't dance to this shit.'

She'd obviously had a few. Somebody pushed past behind her and she fell into him, all warm and sweaty, her mouth close to his ear shouting to be heard above the racket. It was Wham! now, fucking Greek poofters, what else were they going to come up with?

'What kind of music do you like, then?'

'Not this shit, that's for sure.'

'Yeah, but what kind?'

Ray didn't want to tell her. Felt anything he told her would make him vulnerable, but still said: 'I like rock and roll, you know, real rock and roll, Elvis Presley, Chuck Berry, that kind of stuff.'

She laughed.

'You'd get on well with my Dad, you would.'

'What does that mean?'

'He likes all that rubbish.'

'So, obviously your old man's got good taste.'

'Rides a motorbike, too, just like you do.'

'How'd you know I got a bike?'

'My mate Roz said she saw you riding up on it. Bet it's a lot nicer than my Dad's old wreck.'

'It's a Honda, CBR 600.'

Knowing that meant nothing to her.

'My Dad's is a Triumph Bonnerville, best bike ever made, he says, you ever heard of it?'

'All right in its time, the Bonnerville.'

She took him by surprise when she kissed him, her little

warm tongue darting between his teeth, pushing herself against him, Ray wishing he'd bothered to brush his teeth before he came out.

'You going to offer me a lift home then, or what?'

Goodbye Vienna.

Midge Ure.

Somebody ought to have shot that fucking dwarf by now.

'Only if it's right now. I can't take any more of this shit!'

'I'll just tell Roz I'm going.'

Her hand lightly touching the back of his leg.

Like an electric shock…

Joining the A40 just past the American Air Force Base, the Target roundabout, sun coming up, not another soul on the road, getting up to a hundred and twenty-five on the stretch down to Hanger Lane, bodies curved tight together, leaning into the curves…

Fucking magic.

Wrote her phone number, in biro, on the back of his hand.

Ray getting a boner now, just thinking about it, coming off the mini-roundabout at the Queen of England, into the Bath Road, the 600cc engine vibrating between his legs probably having a lot to do with it. Uncomfortable… but pleasurable, like an aching tooth when you worried it with your tongue. If only it could happen that easy with Susanne.

Round her parents' place.

Acton.

Mum tucked up in bed with a good book; Jim, Susanne's old man, through with the six-pack and the Kung Fu movie from the video rental shop, gone up to join her…

Not that there was anything wrong with him. Remembering that time his old lady – before she got sick, started having all the operations – turning the mattress, found the Kleenex tissue, stiff as a board, crinkled like a Smith's crisp packet… 'Dirty bugger,' she had said, 'Don't think I don't know what you've been up to…'

No, no problem in that department.

It had to be Susanne.

Her fault.

Making him nervous.

Hating it when she touched him there.

Before he was ready.

'Why not, Ray, you know I want you to.'

'All I'm saying is we should wait.'

'Don't you know how much I want to make you happy. You're so old fashioned, sometimes.'

'So, what's wrong with being old fashioned?'

'Just relax and stop thinking about it.'

Christ! if it was only that easy, close to tears, not wanting her to put her hand there, feel him like that...

Tell all her friends.

What a laugh!

'How can I relax, your Mum and Dad asleep just up the stairs?'

'Knowing them, I bet they got up to a lot worse than this in their time. What do you think they think we're up to, down here every night?'

'Don't do that.'

'Lots of blokes have this problem, it's not only you.'

Hating it when she came right out and spoke about it like that.

'So, you're the big expert, are you? How come you know so much?'

'Ray, you are such a fool.'

'Is that what you think?'

'I do love you, you know that, don't you?'

'Me, too,' Ray had said.

But he was more certain about the Honda CBR 600 than he was about Susanne. He *knew* he loved the Honda. He went to sleep and woke up thinking about that machine. Thought about winding the rev counter into the red through heavy traffic, finding the gaps, for Ray there was always a gap, like a Japanese Kamikaze pilot, only never having to make the final dive. That CBR didn't eat up the road, it chopped it up into little pieces...

Spat it out.

Like a chainsaw.

With Susanne, it was different. He supposed he loved her. As far as anyone was able to tell for sure, he thought he loved her, accepted it as fact. Certainly, it was on the cards that they would get married at some point, Ray wasn't sure when, everybody just assumed it. Two thousand in the building society was the figure they were aiming at. Susanne put something away every week out of her wages, worked for an accommodation agency along the Gloucester Road, answering the phone. Ray, well there was no use denying – for Ray – money was always a problem. Next year, the year after... nobody was in any hurry to set a date. Susanne's parents were happy enough at the prospect, a right laugh those two, Mrs Dawson – Bette – with her Spanish dance classes, and Jim going through his old records: 'Now clock a listen to this one, Ray, the King at his very peak.' *Good Rockin' Tonight*. 'Collector's item, this EP, worth a few bob, now.'

And the bikes: 'Now *this* is a real man's bike, son, none of those poncey electric starters.'

Ray wishing his bike had a kick-start like Jim's Bonnerville. It did feel good, standing astride the machine, feeling the weight of compression as you kicked down... And as for Ray's parents, they were just happy at the prospect of having Ray off their hands, what with the old lady's illness and Dad having to fetch and carry all the time – Ray wasn't going to miss his cooking, that's for sure.

But, as for love...

At the end of the Bath Road, Ray turned right into The Avenue, then right again into the side-streets of Bedford Park.

Chiswick.

Money.

BMW and Audi territory, second car for the old lady to run the kids around in, probably a Volvo Estate. Second home in the country. Au pairs walking the dog, picking up the youngest from nursery school – you could always spot the au pairs because they were dressed less expensively than the kids they were with.

Cloud cuckoo land.

Well, fuck the lot of them.

Ray slowed to a crawl.

Steep camber, fallen leaves all over the road, didn't want to come off, make an arsehole of himself... spotted a house with a kid's cycle and an old trundle wagon on the porch, pulled into the curb and switched off the ignition.

Ray sat there for a moment, watching a milk float disappear down the road, listening to the tick-tick of the cooling engine, imagining it was talking to him. Then he dismounted, took the hammer out of the pannier and zipped it into the front of his motorcycle jacket.

Giles rang at ten-thirty, like he always did after he'd spent the night with another woman.

Another woman.

Denise thought, Maybe that was the wrong way of putting it. Seven nights in three weeks. That wasn't another woman – that was the *same* woman. It was shaping up into one of those affairs that culminated in Giles packing a bag and leaving for three days before coming home contrite and begging for forgiveness. 'I needed to work it through, you do understand that, Denise, don't you?' Denise wasn't certain that she did understand. Wasn't certain that she was willing to go through that one all over again.

She finished loading the dishwasher, leaving the phone to ring. Let the sod wait!

Who was it the last time? That brainless receptionist at the Magazine, boobies like ogden melons, and happy to advertise the fact. '*London Live!* Can I help you?' In that sing-song whiny Minnie Mouse voice that all telephone receptionists seemed to adopt these days. Denise couldn't stand to ring Giles at the Magazine any more, not when she had to put up with listening to that voice.

'Oh, hi, Denise…' – how could the bitch load so much innuendo into just a name, or was Denise just imagining it? – '…Line's engaged, can you hold?'

And the time before that?

Denise couldn't remember.

Or, rather, she liked to fool herself that she couldn't remember. But, of course, she could. How could she fail to remember when Giles always insisted on recounting every intimate detail – no! sordid detail – like he was a small schoolboy describing to his mother how he had scored the decisive goal in the inter-form cup football match? Confessional? Boasting, more like. As if he actually believed Denise would be impressed. God! She was glad when he had finally decided to part with that old Morris Minor he loved so much. The day couldn't come quick enough for Denise. Still arguing over the replacement, Porsche 911 or Range Rover… symbol of their new affluence. Giles holding out for the Porsche, never willing to accept that he had a small child to accommodate.

Or a wife.

Why had he never made love to *her* in the Morris Minor? Could he ever imagine how she felt when she rode in it? Was it because he knew she would have rejected his advances? Giles! Do stop that. This is all too silly.

That word again.

Silly.

Could it really be *her* fault that he was like he was?

Heaven forbid!

She activated the dishwasher, crossed the kitchen, picked up the receiver: 'Giles?'

'You knew it was me.'

Denise thinking: Of course! People who are predictable don't actually realise they are being predictable – otherwise, they wouldn't be.

Then saying: 'I rather thought it might be.'

'What kept you, were you in the loo, or something?'

'No, I wasn't in the loo, or something.'

'You sound upset. What's the matter?'

'Oh, Giles! You've got a nerve.'

'God! Here we go again.'

'We!'

'I'm sorry, I'm sorry.'

Pause. Denise not wanting to help him fill the silence.

Then: 'Look, last night.'

'Another urgent deadline?'

'We'll have a long chat tonight, over dinner, okay? I don't want to talk about it over the phone, it wouldn't be fair.'

Fair?

That wasn't like Giles. He usually preferred to talk about 'it' over the phone. Face to face, when he was lying, he couldn't help but put on that silly pathetic expression, like he had just wet himself and was hoping the stain didn't show. Denise wondering if he had the same trouble lying to his various women: We're not going to be able to make that trip this Easter after all, Denise is going through a bad time just lately, doctor has prescribed anti-depressants, don't want to come home one night find her in the bath with both her wrists slashed. Of course I don't love her any more but, you have to understand, I do have certain moral obligations. And then there's Mandy to consider…

Did he ever tell them about Mandy? Did he ever tell them about *her* if they didn't already know he was married?

My wife doesn't understand me.

Perhaps it was true.

'Fair? Fair to who, Giles? Me or you?'

'Don't give me a hard time, Denise, please.'

'*Me* give *you* a hard time?'

'Not now, not this morning of all mornings.'

That was more like it.

Giles now going to remind her what it really took to pay the bills, the constant pressure of deadlines, of coming up with something new week after week… how would Giles put it if he was writing a feature: the cost in human terms of being an investigative journalist on a fashionable weekly publication.

The smoke screen.

The diversionary tactic…

The men from the boys; the work hard, play hard scenario. Was it any wonder he sometimes had to blow? Giles had a way of doing that. Turning things around, appealing to his own specific and personal reasoning, making it appear that everything was Denise's fault.

Never his.

'Absolute bloody chaos. Graeme came back unexpectedly – you should see his tan, the bastard – got Chris in his office right now, you can hear them at it all down the corridor.'

Graeme Tate.

The Magazine's publisher.

'I know you've never really liked Chris very much but the word is, his editorship is on the line.'

'Giles, much as I've never had any time for…'

'No, listen…'

'And anyway, I rather had the impression that Graeme was little more than a figurehead these days.'

Since he'd floated the publishing company, became a multi-millionaire, from agit-prop to executive jet, much publicised swanning around with failed television presenter, Helen Monkton, last seen on the small screen documenting the life cycle of the Welsh mussel – Denise stopping herself, wondering why on earth she was allowing herself to be drawn into this.

'That's exactly the mistake Chris made.'

'What?'

'Assuming Graeme was letting go the reins. That hatchet job he ran last week on the Sloane Rangers, 'Hurrah for Henry…''

The mistake Chris made. The feature Chris ran… Giles certainly wasn't wasting any time distancing himself from his bosom buddy, 'You *would* like him, Denise, if you knew him better.' Those interminable late night drinking sessions after the Oasis had finally kicked them out into the street, back at Chris's pied-à-terre, Soho, behind Berwick Street Market, Giles indulging Chris's drunken ramblings, his self-pity, his unwillingness to accept that Elaine had finally left him for good.

Good for Elaine.

Good excuse for Giles.

'So you know Graeme and Helen were out in Mustique, staying with Helen's friend, Bunny Du Cann, got a place on Lord Glenconner's private island, you can imagine what that's worth…'

'Giles…'

'Current edition arrives, special courier, they're all tucking into a champagne lobster breakfast, there's the piece, 'Hurrah for Henry,' photograph of Bunny Du Cann clutching one of his beloved Purdey's all set to blast anything that moves, caption reads, 'The Right Honourable Duncan Du Cann, absent landlord and whisky baron.' Goes on to describe the working conditions at his distillery in Dumfries, starvation wages he pays his work-force… even gets round to that business of why he got kicked out of Marlborough…'

'How embarrassing for Graeme.'

'On the first flight home. I'd hate to be in Chris's shoes right now.'

'Giles…'

How long was this going to go on?

Until Denise put a stop to it.

'…Last night.'

Silence, then, 'I thought we had agreed we'd talk about it later.'

'No, Giles, *you* said we'd talk about it later, but I don't remember my agreeing.'

'Denise, why are you doing this to me?'

'Oh, for God's sake, Giles!'

'Have you become some kind of masochist? Is this some new kinky perversion you are into? What do you want, I should give you a blow by blow account?'

The cornered rat.

Baring its fangs.

'You usually do. What's so different about this time?'

'It's just not important, that's all.'

'Oh, really? Do you want to tell me why?'

'Because it's all over, finished, that's why.'

'Your doing or hers?'

'What a strange question.'

'I don't think so, not under the circumstances. I'd feel rather silly to think I was catching my own husband on the rebound.'

That word, again.

Silly.

'Denise!'

Meaning: How could you say such a thing to me?

And, he probably did think that, too.

'It's not good enough, Giles.'

'We'll talk about it later, work something out.'

'We've done all that before. It never seems to make any difference.'

Wanting to wait…

Hold out till Giles was off the line before she started crying.

'This time it *will* be different. Please, believe me.'

Believe Giles? That was the most silly thing Denise had ever heard.

That word, again.

Silly.

Ray didn't like the woman.

Not one bit.

Snotty bitch, who did she think she was, standing there in that baggy jumper, looked like she'd slept in it, track-suit bottoms, pink plastic sandals? Ray looking at her through the crack in the door, security chain on, her going, 'Ye-es,' stretching the word, loading it enough to say – what on earth could you possibly want at this house?

Knowing he wasn't a Jehovah's Witness, not dressed like that in his motorcycle gear, still wearing his helmet... or one of those kids from up north selling tea towels door-to-door. Perhaps, a motorcycle courier come to the wrong house, there were lots of designers and the like worked from home round this way.

Curiosity turning to doubt.

But no fear.

Not yet.

Ray unzipping his jacket, reaching for the hammer, swinging at the door jamb where the chained was secured. Wood splintering, pushing the door open with his left shoulder, the woman jumping back.

Disbelief.

Ray smiled.

Fear.

Kicking the door closed behind him, turning to secure the dead-bolt, the sliding bolts top and bottom, hearing the other voice, a child's voice, from the top of the stairs, 'Mummy?'

Snotty bitch...

...and her brat.

Curly hair like her mother, just tall enough to reach the banister rail, standing on the first landing, frightened, but frightened to show it.

'God! please don't hurt the child!' Then: 'Just take what you want and go, please!'

Ray ignoring her. Doing what he always did. Pretending he was a deep-sea diver, or an astronaut moon-walking, alone in an alien environment, everything in slow motion, untouchable, Ray entirely separated from his surroundings by the skid-lid and tinted visor, the leather motorcycle suite, the fur-lined flying boots... hearing her voice coming to him, muffled by the protective padding of the crash helmet, like at the swimming baths when water got into your ears.

'Say something!

'For God's sake say something!'

Distant.

'Don't just stand there!'

Ray loving this moment. Loving it more than anything else. More than the Honda CBR 600, even, more than he thought he loved Susanne. The moment they realised not everybody would play by their rules. That, maybe, after all, there were no rules.

He pushed past the woman, taking the stairs three at a time, four long strides, gathered the girl into his arms, the girl unsure whether or not she should begin to cry.

Ray looked down at the woman.

'Now you're not going to do anything stupid, are you?'

It was the woman who started crying.

'So, who was the stud?'

Harry already knowing the answer, Ross having briefed him on the last leg of the journey up through St John's Wood.

'You're weird, you know that, don't you, Harry.'

Harry standing there in a towelling bath-robe, bare feet, just had a long hot soak, bath salts, the works, now feeling a lot better after that long fuck of a journey. Celeste on her hands and knees doing one of those jigsaw puzzles she loved so much, in her housecoat, still not dressed, large gin and tonic, ice cubes and a twist, having difficulty slotting the pieces into place because of the thick pile of the lounge carpet. The jigsaw complete enough for Harry to see a wooden ship with a tall single funnel belching smoke, overshadowed by a larger sailing ship, ghost-like, didn't look finished... who the fuck would pay good money for something that didn't look finished, pull the other one, why don't you?

'Turner,' Celeste said, 'The Fighting Temeraire.'

'Since when did you know anything about paintings?'

'I may not know much about art, Harry, but I can read what it says on a box. The Fighting Temeraire Tugged to her Last Berth... JMW Turner.' Tossing the jigsaw box lid in his direction, Harry stooping to pick it up, the bigger older ship still not looking any more finished in the painting reproduced on the lid. Harry went over to the sofa, sat down, legs splayed, arms spread-eagled along the top of the headrest, still holding the jigsaw box lid.

'Pass it back, will you, Harry, I can't do it without that.'

Celeste draining the gin and tonic, stood up, gave Harry a

look, went over to the bar to fix another drink. Harry noticed she was still walking steady, checked his watch, it was still only eleven-thirty.

Early enough.

'While you're there, build me a scotch and coke, would you.'

'You're home now, Harry. You build bridges; drinks, you mix.'

Celeste poured a small measure of single malt, Isle of Jura, she picked it from the shelf because she liked the shape of the bottle, splash of coke, no ice… Harry didn't like ice with his spirits, liquor – Harry would say, 'The idea is it's supposed to burn, why pour cold water all over it, for Christ's sake?'

'One of these days, you're going to come up with the bright idea of inviting me along with you on one of your trips.'

'You wouldn't like it, stuck on your own all the time, you think I spend my time sight-seeing?'

Celeste handing him his drink, taking the jigsaw lid, waving it like a fan, 'Harry, I have no idea *what* you spend your time doing.'

Sipping from her drink.

Not wanting to get too drunk just yet.

Knowing the question was going to come back.

Wasn't going to go away.

So, who was the stud?

'Tingo Maria.'

'What?'

'Ten days time, you wouldn't like it.'

'Sounds like a drink people don't drink have at Christmas.'

'It's in Peru – you want to tell me about this fuckhead you've been screwing senseless while I've been away?'

'I don't screw around, you know that.'

'I do know that, Celeste, and I don't care… only, this time it's different.'

'You're weirder than I thought.'

'I don't see it that way. I just like my woman to be happy, what's so wrong about that?'

'Plenty I know would beg to differ.'

'You with the prosecution or the defence?'

'Sounds to me I'm in the dock, welcome home, Harry.'

Raising her glass.

Knowing it was a dangerous thing to do.

Harry sensing her fear, not wanting to be the predator, not with Celeste, sitting forward on the sofa, elbows on his knees, scotch and coke held two-fisted, swirling the glass – one thing about no ice cubes, you didn't get that tinkerbell sound when you swirled the glass. 'The fucker's a journalist, didn't you know that?'

'You think I checked his CV?'

Coming back strong.

Maybe, too strong.

'Did you bring him back here?'

'What do you think – we did it in the back of his car?'

'Celeste, I *know* you did it in the back of his car.'

'You know that, then you know I brought him back here.'

'A fucking journalist nosing around in my house!'

The house that Harry built.

'You want it straight, Harry, we were too busy screwing for him to have time to be nosing around the house.'

'I need to be certain.'

'So, how will you manage that?'

'Piece of piss – I'll ask him.'

Celeste struggling to take it all in. Harry knew, probably, had always known, but didn't care. Needed to get into some clothes. Go upstairs, take a shower, put on her face, be more prepared for Harry in this kind of mood. What the fuck did he care Giles was a journalist?

'I need to go and dress, Harry.'

Jeans.

T-shirt.

Nothing fancy.

Harry not reading her mind, just knowing her well enough, saying, 'Do me a favour, Celeste, put on something nice... that black number you picked up in Italy, you haven't worn that for a while.'

'Italy? That was five years ago, Harry.'

Harry hated jeans. Never wore them himself. Could never work out what was the big attraction, that old pair Celeste was so fond of, looked like she was never going to throw out, frayed pockets, knees poking through, why the fuck, money he gave her for clothes. Women in jeans reminded Harry of those scrubbers you saw down the Mile End Road, waiting for the overnight lorry drivers, hanging around outside McDonalds, after the pubs had turned out, hair down to their arses...

Harry holding it right there.

That wasn't Celeste...

Not in a million years.

'It was just a thought.'

Celeste kicked out at the jigsaw, scattering the pieces, a section of the ghost ship left there on the carpet, making no sense whatever without it's outline, grey, like a storm cloud, nobody knew how to paint the edges

'Promise me you don't ever see him again.'

'Fuck you, Harry, what is this?'

Harry not sure he could explain, even if he had wanted to. A safe pair of hands, he had always prided himself on that. The Tingo Maria connection on the telephone, long distance, a bunch of greasers now seeing him as a loose cannon. Fuck knows what the kid might have dug up, Celeste sleeping off a session, World War Three wouldn't wake her. Imagining the conversation, Nestor or Ramon saying, 'We got the London editions here, Harry, it don't look good.' Harry, on the defensive, 'No sweat, nothing I can't handle.' 'Maybe, now is not such a good time. No disrespect, Harry, but we should wait till this thing blows over.' Harry knowing this was a crock of shit. That they would never get back to him. Ever. Thinking he should ring Bertram right now, have him come over, go through the paperwork, check how much of it could be incriminating, see if anything was missing, find out what exactly the kid could have come away with given Celeste hadn't fucked out *all* his brain cells.

The scotch kicking in.

Jet lag.

Empty stomach.

Harry laughing.

Thinking: Ease off, Harry. Who the fuck needed Bertram round here going through the books, first morning back with Celeste.

Saying, 'When was it, Celeste?'

'When was what?'

Knowing what he meant.

That look on Harry's face, sat there on the sofa.

Who needed hard to get?

'Twenty-two days, two hours,' glance at her watch, 'twenty-seven minutes... right after Ross packed your bags in the car, sat out there waiting with the engine running.'

Not sure about the minutes, but knowing it would please Harry.

'So, what's new?'

'He was twenty-seven, Harry. You think he would know something you don't?'

'Kids today, who knows?'

Astride Harry's lap, Celeste's knees deep into the sofa, working on getting Harry uncomfortable, then, her hand guiding him to the one place it wouldn't hurt. Harry sighing, then losing it. Celeste, her hand in Harry's mouth, offering him her fingers one by one, Harry biting each one just enough to hurt, knowing she liked that, watching her head down between his legs, dressing gown open, thinking about Nestor and Ramon, the South Side club, night before he flew home, business settled, Ramon saying, 'Let's have ourselves a good time, Harry.'

Nestor saying, 'In the normal way of things, Harry, this would not be such a great movie. The guy, he's in too much of a hurry, doesn't let her see it coming, you know what I mean?'

Snuff movie.

Ramon adding, 'She doesn't see it coming, what's the fucking point?'

Woman in her early-twenties, white bridal gown, white veil, bunch of red roses, coming down the aisle, priest stood there waiting with a bible open in his hands.

'This sister, she never did anything like this before, old man up for armed robbery, murder-one on two counts, got a sick kid and a habit to support, not expensive, but now more than she can afford... guy says he can maybe help her out she does him this small favour, fucking incredible!'

The priest has his pecker out, the bride is now on her knees, takes it into her mouth, working on it.

'Now, this is where the script changes, only the sister, she don't know that.'

The priest, '... in sickness and in health... to love, honour and obey...'

Taking a thirty-eight Cobra out from underneath his cassock, pointing it down at the top of the woman's head, she hasn't seen a thing, too busy still working on his pecker.

'Catch this, Harry. This is what makes this such a great movie... man, you any idea how much copies of this change hands for?'

Pulls the trigger as he comes. The woman's head explodes, white wedding dress and red roses, you can't now tell them apart, wedding dress crumpled on the floor as if there was nobody in it, the priest quick-stepping backwards in a Michael Jackson moon-dance routine, screaming, clutching himself, pumping blood...

Nestor, Ramon, everybody in the club laughing hysterically, 'You dig that, man,' Ramon saying... 'Dumb fucker just blew away his own pecker.'

Let's have ourselves a good time, Harry.

Harry wanting to throw up.

Celeste, given up trying, looking up into Harry's face.

'What is it, Harry?'

Reaching up, putting her arms round him, her face close to his.

Holding Harry tight.

'Stay like that, will you, Celeste?'

'Long as you want, Harry,' Celeste said.

The woman was crying again.

Not wailing, like the racket she'd been making at first, outside in the hall, before he's come down the stairs, still holding the kid, slapped her one round the face. These were deep sobs, regular as a heartbeat, but half time, like the King when he sang, 'One – night – with – you,' or, the verse Ray preferred: 'Just – call – my – name... And I'll be there by your side,' just like Ray was now with this woman, only she was saying, 'What... do... you... want?'

Over and over, in that same rhythm the King used in that song, arms folded across her chest, trying to keep herself covered up, despite Ray's instructions. The jumble sale tat spread all over the floor where she'd dropped it, dining room, big wooden polished table, lots of chairs round it, you could feed an army, the table top covered with letters, bills, kids' colouring books, toys, she wasn't much for the housework that was for sure… Ray's Mum would have had a fit, state this place was in, a right tip.

'Why are you humiliating me?' Breaking the rhythm, getting it all out in one breath now, before going back to the sobs.

Magic.

'Did I touch you?'

'You hit me!'

'You asked for it, screaming like that.'

Ray surprised how good she looked, had to be pushing forty if she was a day, maybe there already. Slim, pale, nice gap at the top of her thighs, like that model, Twiggy, always all over the papers when he was a kid. 'Bag of bones,' Ray's Mum used to say: 'What any man could see in her, I don't know.' Not like Susanne – not that Ray had ever seen her with all her clothes off, but you could tell. Nobody could ever accuse Susanne of being slim.

'You should make more of yourself, you know that?'

Noticing the stretch marks.

The kid not moving, still in his arms. Ray gave her a squeeze, her head banging into the side of his crash helmet, but not hard enough to hurt. She still hadn't cried. Big eyes, wide, purple through the tinted visor.

'See what you did to your Mum.'

Giving her another hug.

The girl stiff in his arms, acting as if she hadn't even heard him.

'Please…' the woman said.

Ray smiled.

That was nice.

Please…

A phone was ringing. From down the hall. Echoing around the varnished floors, the emulsioned walls, bouncing from room to room.

Ray put the kid down.

'Don't…' the woman said.

'Don't what?'

The phone stopped ringing.

Chapter 3

She swallowed the cat,
To catch the bird…

Ross liked to talk to Mary over the phone. Any time, night or day, just hearing her voice, soft as rain, imagine her young and beautiful again. Beautiful as the day he made the trip over to Cork to declare his intentions, her old man saying, 'We'll go for a quart in The Swan.' Beautiful as the Chandon Bells the day they married, beautiful as the young girl in the photographs she liked to show him, teasing him, 'Do you see what you missed, Ross, coming so late into my life?' Before she came across the water, shared digs in North London, got a job as a waitress in the Kordoma Cafe, Edgware Road, just off Marble Arch, living on tips – till she met Ross. Walked in one day, mid-afternoon, tea, two sugars, took a table for four, three empty seats, still looking like he didn't have room to breath…

And that was it.

Mary had been forty when they married, Ross twenty-five.

'Fifteen years, Ross,' Mary had said. 'Will you think about it?'

Ross now forty, himself.

Listening to her voice.

Still thinking about it.

'Have to go, Mary. Found a meter.'

Leinster Square, rain coming down, cold and grey, a bay with enough extra to take Harry's Roller, two feet stolen from a Mini Clubman, three from a builder's Transit, nearside wheel on the curb, back end saying, 'What the fuck,' to oncoming traffic.

'What about dinner?'

Magic gone.

'Mary?'

'What does that mean, "Mary?"'

'You know Harry just got back.'

'You should learn to say "no" sometimes, Ross.'

White BMW, current plates, coming round Ross, reverse lights showing, 'No fucking way,' Ross saying to himself, easing forward, picturing how big his bonnet must look in the fuckhead's rear view mirror, thinking, Back off, I don't need this.

Mary on the phone, 'Harry this, Harry that, he doesn't own you, Ross.'

BMW, window sliding down to give the finger before accelerating away.

Ross thinking, Your lucky day.

Saying, again, 'Mary?'

Mary saying, 'I'll leave it in the oven.'

Ross reversing into the bay, rain coming down heavier, now, windows fogged. Feeding the meter and cursing Harry. Thirty-five minutes to park the Roller, wheel-base the size of a fucking bus. Up before dawn, waiting for Harry to come down, drive him up to Hampstead, and now The Brewer to sort... Mary still asleep, he'd been up four hours already, could have been tucked up close, Mary whispering, 'Do you think this is right, Ross, us still doing this, me at my age?' Fifty-five. 'Don't you sometimes wish you were with a younger woman?' Mary, his whole life since he had walked into the Kordoma all those years ago, thinking, now, Any other time, fuck the double-yellows, park the motor out front of The Duke, let Bertram take care of the paperwork, that's what he was there for...

But, not this time.

You could hardly not notice a Roller, coachwork like a Chevy, blocking the left turn from Queensway into Westbourne Grove, The Brewer climbing into the passenger seat, office workers on their lunch-break, heads down against the rain, clutching their sandwiches, one of them ringing the filth, 'This may not be important, but...'

Ross cutting across Leinster Square, right on Westbourne Grove, making a mental note to bring this up with Harry, pick up something smaller, less obvious. Trouble was, Harry thought he was doing Ross a big favour letting him ride around in the Roller, and it wasn't worth it, not if Harry was going to get offended.

Ross pushed through the heavy double doors into the bar, glad to be out of the rain. There were leaded lights in the doors,

Private Bar etched in glass, but the Duke of Wellington had long-since been knocked though into one bar, refurbished in red leatherette, brass fittings, pin table and fruit machine, both in use, making the usual racket, place full of tourists – how come, today, Ross couldn't manage to keep away from fucking tourists? Looked around for The Brewer, not expecting to see him. The Brewer, otherwise known as 'The Droop', Adrian only to his mother, Mrs Limbrick, always late. Ross ordering a coffee at the bar, New Zealand kid in a red velvet waistcoat saying, 'Sorry, sir, we don't serve coffee during the lunch period, too busy.' Ordered a glass of pale ale instead, sat at the bar, watching the tourists go through their guide books, diet cokes sat on the table, hardly touched, working out where to risk going for lunch.

'You think it will be clean?'

Blue-collar from Milwaukee. Staying at one of those tarted-up Victorian joints, hundreds of them opening up the other side of Queensway, coaches double-parked everywhere you looked.

'They take AmEx, it says here, Dorothy… it should be okay, they take AmEx.'

'Well, I don't know, Homer…

'Dorothy, we got to eat someplace!'

The Whiteness Hotel.

That was Ross's favourite. Stroke of pure genius, that name.

Could you just picture Dorothy and Homer back home, five thousand miles away, some suburb used to be part of the Western Plain, sifting through the literature, Homer resigned to the fact that he was finally going to have to make the trip over to Europe this summer… 'This looks good, Homer, The Whiteness Hotel – clean, no coloureds – 'just ten minutes from Oxford Street,' – accent on the 'ford', as in fording a river, making a connection no Olde Worlde Londoner would ever have considered – 'five minutes from The Royal Gardens of Kensington,' – maybe bump into Her Royal Highness, The Queen of England, out taking a stroll with Philip?

Ten minutes from Oxford Street, five minutes from The Royal Gardens of Kensington – and two minutes from Westbourne Park and Paddington, Homer, and all the low-life users and abusers, pimps and schoolgirls just in from Wales and the north you could ever hope to meet up with on a dark night in one lifetime, or that Dorothy could ever dream of in her wildest nightmares…

Ross chuckling.

You had to hand it to them.

'You think there's a McDonalds?'

'Homer, there's always a McDonalds.'

A hand on Ross's shoulder.

'So, how's my favourite Paddy today, then, Ross?'

Every time…

Every time, he said that.

Then, to the kid behind the bar, 'Tennents Extra, pint, if you would be so kind. Ross, can I get you a top up?'

Ross covering his glass with his hand, shaking his head, 'We need to be away.'

'Suit yourself.'

The Brewer, taking his time over the Tennents Extra, telling Ross the one – swore it was a true story – about the Irishman on a transatlantic flight, jumbo 747, coming back from the smoking section, passes one of the galley stations, hears a hostess shovelling ice into a bucket… pulls back the curtain, says, 'Fook, I didn't realise these things ran on steam,' pleased as punch with the 'Fook', genuine Irish, expecting Ross to laugh.

'You get it, Ross? She's shovelling ice, dumb fucker hears it, thinks she's shovelling coal, just picture it, all those hostesses stoking the furnace like mad to keep the fucker in the air.'

'Drink your drink, Brewer,' Ross said.

The Brewer, aka The Droop, aka Adrian Limbrick, south London grammar school boy made good, born into the drug culture, the age of hippydom, marijuana, acid, speed – quit the civil service when casual dealing became a full time occupation. Who needed to work for a living, money he was making? Moved on into hard drugs, attracted serious attention, settled for a percentage, what other choice did he have? The Brewer was moving fourteen grammes every week. A quarter gramme gave you three ten pound 'bags'. One hundred and sixty-eight bags, that was one thousand six hundred and eighty pounds…

Sterling.

Cash in hand.

Inland Revenue could go fuck themselves.

Not bad for a working class kid, was passing out giros, DHSS Office, Wandsworth, just three years back…

Only, you could never trust a user.

And Harry hadn't built his reputation passing uncut cocoa.

Ross watched Homer arguing with his wife, Dorothy, over whether they should leave the 'barkeep' a tip, decided against it...

Left to go check out some old walls.

Coach trip to Arundel Castle.

'Finish that, will you?'

The Brewer still taking his time over the lager, saying, 'You know, Ross, for a Paddy, you're a bundle of laughs.'

Ross wanting to smack him in the face, there, right that moment. Imagine the fucker swallowing teeth, poison himself, state they were in.

Only, Harry had other plans...

Denise concentrating on the chores, trying not to think about Giles on the phone this morning, their conversation. A sudden absence of sound, autowash cycle complete: taking the smalls to the upstairs airing cupboard, sorting them, hers, Giles's, Mandy's. Draining the upstairs bathroom sink, where her 'period' knickers had been soaking, wringing them, taking them downstairs along with the two bath towels, knickers in the tumble drier, towels out to the washing line in the back garden. Noticing how well the honeysuckle had done this summer, the blossom now fallen, remembering the pervasive aroma of the flowers.

'Like a bordello,' Giles had said, but what would he know? Denise could never imagine Giles needing to go to a place like that, and he certainly wasn't the sort to pay for anything when he didn't have to... When had she planted the honeysuckle? Three years, four? Now, almost taken over the back wall of the house, reaching up to Mandy's window on the first floor. So fast, almost as if, if you watched closely, you would be able to see it grow.

She thought that way of Mandy, too.

Growing so fast.

Thinking, despite herself: if it had been Barbara had paired off with Giles that Easter college trip to Paris, that night in the hotel near the Gard du Nord, *she* wouldn't have become pregnant, married…

Trapped.

Not Barbara.

She'd gone with…? Not able to remember the boy's name. Nice eyes, she could remember his eyes, long hair past his shoulders, spoke French fluently, his father something important in UNESCO, moved about a lot as a child… Stuart! That was it. See, she could remember. Denise wondering, if it *had* been the other way around, not following meekly in Barbara's footsteps, like she always did, standing by while Barbara took off with Stuart, leaving her with Giles…

Looked like rain, but decided to risk leaving the towels. Didn't want them in with her knickers.

Realising what she was doing.

Blaming Barbara for her life with Giles.

How bloody pathetic!

Checking the fridge. Giles's risotto from last night, the dinner he hadn't bothered to come home to eat. Should she prepare something special as they were going to talk? No, sod it. The risotto would do. Wishing, suddenly, that there was somebody she could talk to… really talk to.

Jane?

Well, she was all right in small doses.

Marriage, careers, the expense of remaining in London, had all taken their toll of the friendships that had survived through school and art college. Promises to keep in touch broken. Names on a once-a-year Christmas card with a hurriedly scribbled note. There was only Barbara. And she was in Wales.

Thinking again of Jane, Denise wondering if there really was such a thing as a new friend, a relationship not forged in the shared experiences of growing up? Pictured herself arriving on Jane and Peter's doorstep with Mandy and a suitcase: 'Sorry to presume, but would it be okay if Mandy and I stayed for a while, just till we can get ourselves sorted out?'

'Why, of course, you poor dears… Oh, really? Well, I can't say it comes as any surprise. Peter! Peter, darling, guess what? But for how long could it be expected to last, the *bonhomie*, the goodwill, the hospitality? The upwardly mobile were constantly moving on, couldn't afford to carry dead weight.

Herself and Mandy.

Dead weight.

Nearly out of washing-up liquid, better make a note.

Incredible!

Realising how absolutely dependent she had become on Giles. *His* money, *his* lifestyle, *his* job, *his* friends. No life of her own. Only Mandy, keeping house, and Jane's endless prattle every afternoon when she brought Mandy home.

'I just don't believe that Kate is being stretched enough at that school. Do you know, she wakes up crying in the night, wanting me to read to her? Of course she's frustrated, of course she's difficult, sometimes...'

Of course!

Barbara.

It would be so easy. Pack a bag, ring for a minicab, collect Mandy from school on the way. Which station was it for Aberystwyth, Paddington? Could be there by early evening, call Barbara to come and pick them up from the station, wouldn't she be surprised... no, delighted. In her last letter, Barbara had described the Old Rectory – she had been there six months now – it was high time Denise came down to see how lovely it all was, the apple orchard, the stream at the end of the garden, the view of the mountains, Denise would love it.

But would Barbara love it, having Denise and Mandy there for an unlimited period, and with all their problems...?

Of course she would.

Barbara was a real friend, would be only too happy to help Denise escape a marriage of which she had always heartily disapproved.

'You have your own life to lead, Denise. If Giles needs a housekeeper so badly, let him pay for one, he can afford it now, money he earns on that magazine...' Reminding her of what their graphics tutor at art college had said, 'An innate sensitivity towards your subject.' '...You were always more gifted than Giles, why do you chose to forget that?' Denise home looking after the baby, Giles getting the job on *London Live!*, paste-up artist, 'not much, but it's a start.' They'd got a baby-sitter in, gone out to Pizza Express in Wardour Street to celebrate, the original Pizza Express. Then Giles getting involved with that girl in features – involved, now an entirely different connotation – researching chauvinism in London restaurants, out four nights a week for God knows how many weeks. Other assignments followed, Chris offering him the job in editorial, making it official. 'Forget the cow gum, Giles, the art department can learn to live without you.' You didn't have to be a gifted graphic designer to be an investigative journalist. You didn't have to be a gifted graphic designer to be a housewife and mother, either.

'Abort,' Barbara had said, when Denise told her.

Abort?

Mandy?

Perhaps she had meant Giles.

Barbara always so definite in her opinions: a *lack* of innate sensitivity towards her subject? Yet, despite, or maybe because of this, Denise had always felt a need to impress her, admired her successful career as an illustrator, never allowing personal relationships to get in the way, working regularly for The United States, book covers, advertising commissions, her originals selling well through galleries in New York and Austin, Texas.

Impress Barbara?

How on earth could she hope to do that, with her mundane existence, her lack of decisiveness?

That night with Jack, after the party, had *that* been to impress Barbara? Some gauche exercise to demonstrate that, despite being married to Giles, despite Mandy, she could still be a free spirit? Certainly, Barbara had played no small part in setting it up, sensing the chemistry between them, or had she been attempting to do more than that? Instigate a breakdown between her and Giles. If she went to Wales, she was bound to bump into Jack, wouldn't be able to avoid it. It was a small incestuous community and it wouldn't take long for Jack to learn that she was staying with Barbara, had left Giles.

Denise wasn't ready for that.

Wasn't sure she could handle it.

Not yet.

Oh, God! Is that the time, already? Jane will be back with Mandy soon. Don't want to leave them on the doorstep.

That only left Mother.

'How could you have…? With that spineless little fool? Your whole life ahead of you and now look what you've let yourself in for!'

No, she couldn't.

'Just don't come crying to me, my girl, that's all.'

Wouldn't.

Denise wanted to ring Giles back at the Magazine, just to talk to him, just to talk to anybody. About anything. But, she would have to put up with that silly little bitch on reception saying, *'London Live!* How can I help you?'

Shopping list. Better get a move on.

A memory came to her.

It should have been funny.

But wasn't.

Denise, suddenly aware of Giles, there in the bedroom. She had fallen asleep with her book still open, Iris Murdoch... *A Severed Head*. Giles reaching to turn out the bedside light without waking her.

'What time is it?'

'I thought you were asleep.'

How was it, she could remember the book she was reading?

'I was.'

Giles, very drunk, having trouble taking his jeans off standing up. Denise putting the light back on, taking a while to register what it was that was wrong.

Different.

'Giles, you have your underpants on back to front.'

A statement.

Not a question.

Because even Giles couldn't come up with an answer to that one.

Yesterday's risotto.

Oh, God.

Then aware that the phone was ringing, had been for some time.

Bertram was seething – upset with Harry, really upset this time. Who did he think he was, talking to him like that? Staring at the phone sitting there on his desk, half expecting it to jump back off the cradle, hear Harry's voice barking down the line, giving him, him for Christ's sake, a hard time.

Watching the women across the street on the first floor,

stripping to their underclothes, trying on a dress, then trying on another one, preening in front of the mirror. A regular peepshow, if you liked that kind of thing, you'd have thought a big store like that could have come up with something a little more private for changing. Traffic on Regent Street at a standstill, motorcycle couriers hell bent on self-destruction, take a few pedestrians with them, pavements crowded with tourists. The hydraulic hoists would be round soon, Christmas lights going up, they got earlier every year. Bertram having a quiet fit at the prospect. Christmas, God, he hated Christmas. Couldn't get a quiet drink or a quiet meal out for love or money...

Hearing Harry say, again: 'Do yourself a favour, Bertram, lay off the sulphates.'

Saying: 'Don't tempt me, Bertram. Next time you throw a moody, hand in your notice, I might just accept it.'

Saying: 'Just do it, for fuck's sake!'

It wasn't fair.

Bertram's job was the paperwork.

That was the deal.

So, all right, to a point, he could see what Harry was on about. He wasn't exactly hard done by. No clocking in, no clocking out, Sarah, sitting there right now at the other desk pruning her nails, applying the varnish, type a letter, pop down to Brewer Street for a sandwich, you asked her nicely; his own fridge stocked up with low-cal preservative-free real fruit yoghurt, his own toilet, own key, bleach and Harpic Mountain Pine charged to the company...

And the money.

Cash in hand.

No questions asked.

Standing there in the fourth floor bay window, watching the women changing. Two room office, him and Sarah, two desks and the paperwork in one, sofa, easy chairs, colour TV, fish tank with a goldfish wouldn't die – the other room for visitors, only they never had any visitors apart from Harry and Ross, didn't even have a nameplate on the intercom downstairs.

Harry saying, 'The fuck I need to know about this.'

Never interested in detail, especially with Bertram trying to bring him up to date after he'd been away on a trip. The auditors querying additional survey fees, The Walton Riverside Development, twelve grand unaccounted.

'They want to see invoices, Harry. What am I supposed to tell them, it came out of petty cash?'

'Tell them what the fuck you want.'

'It's not that easy.'

'So find a new auditor.'

'This isn't *our* auditor, Harry, this is the Inland Revenue.'

'Bertram, this shit is what I pay you for.'

Bertram in full, never 'Bert'. Harry was okay in some ways. Like that time Sarah was off sick, some female problem or other, temp complained to Harry she might catch AIDS breathing the same air as Bertram all day long, Harry kicking her fat backside down the stairs, all four flights. And that big bunch of white lilies at Gerry's funeral, he hadn't needed to do that... but, that was Harry, always full of surprises.

And always called him Bertram.

Wondering how Harry would react...

He knew Bertram was a second name, after his parents' first born, the older brother Bertram never knew, died at birth – that his actual first name was Danté, as in Danté the Italian writer, wrote *The Commedia*; or Danté Gabriel Rossetti, threw all his poetry into his wife's grave as a grand gesture after she OD'd, came back later and dug it up. Danté, the cross Bertram had to bear, hippy parents, dragged through the mud at the Isle of White and Glastonbury, his formative years spent listening to Bob Dylan squawk into a microphone.

No way...

Danté.

...knowing Harry wouldn't give a flying fuck.

Looking at the phone number Harry had given him at the start of the call, before the altercation, before Bertram had started talking lines of demarcation and Harry said, 'Just do it, for fuck's sake!'

Nine-nine-five.

A Chiswick prefix.

Sarah, through with the nail polish, saying, 'Everything all right, you and Harry?'

'It will blow over.'

Told Sarah to go take a break, get herself some lunch.

'Bring you back something?'

'Just a coffee would be nice. Cappuccino, make sure they remember the chocolate.'

Waited till he could no longer hear her footsteps on the stairs, then dialled the number.

Harry only slept for four hours, then Celeste heard him moving around upstairs, taking another shower, then on the phone in his 'office', box room off the first floor landing, giving Bertram a hard time about something... voice raised, shouting. That wasn't like Harry. Harry spoke soft, *that's* when you knew you had a problem.

Celeste was at the kitchen table, scrubbed pine, bare feet cold on the tiled floor, staring at the rain through the French windows, looking out across the landscaped garden, gazebo in the distance, she'd never ever walked that far. Lighting another Dunhill, using a saucer as an ashtray, pissed off at the way Harry's homecoming had turned out, not wanting to think about it, counting the fancy pots and pans hanging from hooks on the kitchen wall, expensive imported stuff from Habitat, you had to be a weight-lifter to even think of picking one of them up.

'Just don't get the idea you're marrying me for my cooking,' Celeste had said, when Harry told her – didn't ask, just told her – they were going to get married.

Tim in the ground just three weeks.

Accidental death.

Malfunction, lift in some hotel Harry and Tim were staying at in The Hague, the two of them in Holland on a business trip both of them were excited as kids about. Doors open, Tim walks out into empty space, falls twelve floors on to the roof of the lift, still on the ground floor, trust Harry to book the penthouse suite. The two of them going all the way back to cracking heads in the school playground together, just getting comfortable with success...

Fucking crazy.

Harry saying, 'It's not your cooking I want to marry you for, Celeste.' Celeste saying they maybe ought to wait awhile, anyway, Harry saying, 'Tim would have liked it... you think he would have wanted us walking around in sackcloth?'

'Black, Harry, you wear black when somebody dies.

Sackcloth is when you're some fucking religious nut, can't stop playing with yourself.' Soon as you're dead, Celeste thinking, Everybody becomes an expert on what you would have liked...

Through with the Funnies in last week's *Mail on Sunday*, decided against another cup of Maxwell House, ate the last of the toast and cottage cheese, some breakfast, the Funnies reminding Celeste of what Giles had said about how *The Beano* had always been his favourite comic, still bought it now and then, for old times sake. 'The whole punk movement,' Giles saying, 'Malcolm McClaren got his inspiration for the whole punk movement from Dennis's dog, Gnasher... that expression, the collar.'

'Malcolm who?' Celeste had said.

In some cheap Indonesian Restaurant, Highgate Road, just up from Kentish Town, 'You don't have to do this, you know, Giles. Take me out for meals. It's not as if we were going out or anything.'

'I like it, us doing things together.' Her very own Little Plum, throwing up warning signals, Celeste reading them loud and clear. Giles making a fool of himself playing macho-man with a green chilli came with the spinach dish, eyes watering, Celeste laughing. Then, afterwards, back at the house, fucking each other senseless – no, not that night... that night Celeste had gone down on him, blown Giles slow and easy, wanted him to return the favour only Giles didn't like to do that, selfish bastard! Celeste settling for guiding his hand to where it would drive her nuts, which was okay, too ... Giles getting it on just as she was coming, turning her over, taking her from behind, doggy fashion...

Well, okay, maybe they had fucked each other senseless.

Harry was standing in the kitchen door.

More relaxed.

Looking pleased with himself.

'Fucking Peruvians.'

'Not like you, Harry, you don't usually let things get on top of you.'

'I've got no choice in this. I don't get involved, some other fucker will.'

As much as he'd ever talked about business.

Ever...

'Taking it out on Bertram isn't going to help.'

'You don't think so?' When Harry smiled, it was like you wouldn't recognise him from the photograph, going through customs. 'Bertram is an old woman. He needs a good kick up the arse, occasionally.'

'And the rest.'

'Spare me the details.'

Despite the smile, Celeste still not sure of Harry's mood. 'Harry, I'm worried about you, you know that?'

'Don't ever be scared of me, Celeste.'

Celeste ignoring that one, afraid to admit to herself that she *was* scared, eighth anniversary coming up in three months, February, and suddenly she couldn't read Harry any more. 'Like this morning, that's not like you at all, Harry. Long as I've known you, you never had any problem in that direction.'

Playing with her empty coffee cup. Wishing she had a tumbler of G&T in front of her, ice to the top.

'We're none of us getting any younger.'

'Tell me about it.'

'*Young Blood*, you remember that song, The Marauders?'

'The Coasters, Harry. The Marauders was, *That's What I Want*.'

Harry saying, not even trying to sing: 'I don't want your money, I don't want your gold…'

Celeste: 'All I want is a love that's true.'

Harry: 'All I want is you.'

Both of them remembering the exact moment, party in Streatham, Celeste wearing a blue gingham dress, Harry his best blue mohair, white button down, chisel shoes. Celeste a non-drinker back then, a glass of Babycham – Babycham, for fuck's sake! – Harry with a half bottle of White Horse, fitted neat into his inside pocket…

Cheek to cheek.

Another eight years before they were married.

Harry always saying, 'I want it to be right, Celeste. You're too special for it to be any other way.'

The last of the Babycham drinkers saying, now, 'Harry…'

Wanting to go to him, hold him in her arms like the big baby she always used to think he was… not able to move from the chair.

'You want to know the truth, Harry? It's because, when you're away, I miss you too fucking much, that's why.'

'I know that.'

Harry still standing in the doorway, like a repairman, come to fix the dishwasher, not sure if it was the right time...

A big kid.

Harry's favourite photograph, framed and hanging on the bedroom wall; Harry and Tim, arms around each other's shoulders, standing in front of a bell tent, Boy's Brigade uniforms, short trousers, summer camp, Bognor Regis, every year the same two weeks. Tearaways frozen in time. Harry telling her about his friend Tim, before she met him: 'Brought up right next door to each other, street got knocked down in the fifties, you know that stretch at the start of the M4, between Hammersmith Flyover and Chiswick Roundabout? You could say me and Tim were born in the fast lane...' Laughing.

But, not now.

'Be angry with me for the right reasons, Harry.'

'How do you mean?'

'You don't mind, except he was a journalist?'

'You think there's some other reason?'

Celeste not knowing why she should say it, wishing straight away she hadn't. 'Go fuck yourself, Harry,' she said.

'You never been tempted?'

'End up like you?'

'I do all right.'

'Is that what you think?'

The Brewer's flat, Barons Court mews, first floor above a garage that stayed empty apart from all the cardboard boxes and polystyrene packing The Brewer's hi-fi equipment had arrived in, fuck knows why he hung on to all that packaging, maybe to prove it was legit if the Filth came knocking. The Brewer didn't like cars, couldn't tell a clutch pedal from a carburettor, and then there was the hassle of tax, insurance, getting ripped off by some cowboy mechanic, sharp intake of breath, 'It's a big job, then there's the parts, it's going to cost...'

Ross had heard it all before, thankful that this would be the last time, looking out over the cobbled mews, nice displays of hyacinths in wooden tubs, Porsche and a bottle green Range

Rover parked up like they belonged, thinking The Brewer would have no trouble affording this – two hundred a week, twenty-five-year lease – especially now he was dealing shit, cutting to nothing, fucking Harry's reputation.

Three rooms, bedroom, kitchen, living room, small bathroom with a shower unit off the bedroom… the living room furnished in tubular steel, black leather finish, nothing you could relax in. White emulsion walls, rush matting, big Sony colour TV, a single poster on the wall, Madonna, 'Italians Do It Better', folding down at the left top corner where the Blue-tac had come unstuck. The stereo system, all expensive stuff, laser turntable, CD-player, twin cassette deck, linear speakers, must have cost a small fortune. CDs and albums wall to wall.

'Don't have *Danny Boy*, Ross, maybe some Laurie Anderson?'

Selected a CD.

Keeping the volume low – Ross could still hear the District and Piccadilly Line trains coming through, more Piccadilly than District, the District Line trains groaning like tired work horses as they pulled out of Barons Court station, still hear the traffic ticking over, moving slowly along the Cromwell Road, the occasional car zipping by at the end of the mews, knew the rat run through to the North End Road.

Ross had parked the Roller two blocks away.

'We catch a bus from here, or what?'

'There might not be anything nearer.'

'And here was me hoping to impress the neighbours.'

Now, in the flat, Ross saying, 'You have to do that in here?'

'You know the routine, Ross. My old man used to tell me, never trust a spade or a Paddy, no matter what.'

'Short jocks?'

'Yeah, them too. In fact, especially, short jocks.'

'Your old man was right. Why don't you use the bathroom?'

'I like you to see what you're missing.'

The Brewer broke the tape on the cellophane pack with a penknife. Using the flat of the blade he spooned some powder from the pack into a desert spoon, resting the spoon on the glass-topped table where Ross had dumped the packet. He went into the kitchen, Ross hearing a drawer slide open, then shut, not sliding easy. The Brewer came back in holding a fresh ten-pack of one-mil syringes, broke one out.

'Thank the Lord for diabetes, eh, Ross.' Went out again, came back, this time with a brown glass bottle containing vitamin C powder, put it down on the table, next to the dessert spoon.

'I like to use a lemon,' giving Ross the full performance, 'Fresh out of the fuckers.' Went out to the kitchen one last time and poured a glass of tap water.

Ross had seen junkies shooting up using malt vinegar, filter from a used butt, taken from an ashtray, rusty needle, direct into the corner of the eyeball. He wasn't impressed with The Brewer's ritual... he just wanted it over with.

The Brewer placed a matchbox under the handle of the spoon to steady it, shook a little of the vitamin C powder around the circumference of the smack, drew some water from the glass into the syringe and fed it gently into the spoon. Then he picked up the spoon, warmed the bowl briefly with the flame from his lighter, put the spoon back down, and stirred the mixture with his penknife.

Golden brown.

Golden eye.

The Brewer then placed a small wad of cotton wool into the bowl of the spoon, watched it absorb the liquid, at the same time, using a tie, he knotted a tourniquet round his left arm, gripping the end of the tie hard in his left hand. Moving faster now... Held up the syringe, licked the tip, placed it in the soaked filter, released the plunger. Cleared the air, found a good vein at the base of his thumb, missed the first time.

'Shit!'

Second attempt, drawing some blood into the syringe, making certain he had found the vein, pressed home the plunger... all the way.

Said, 'Shit!'

A second time.

This time, with a whole different meaning.

'You just did the world a big favour, Brewer,' Ross said.

'No, man, I just did me a big favour.'

Releasing the tourniquet, dumping the syringe in a wastebin under the table.

'Good stuff.'

Thick bastard.

'Pure.'

'No shit.'

The Brewer didn't care.

Ross did... this was too easy.

Gaucho'd.

'Tell me another joke, Brewer...'

The Brewer stretching out in the chair, legs spread-eagled, head back, finding something to study on the ceiling. 'Two paddies on a jet, right... pilot keeps coming through announcing another engine has gone, that their arrival time is going to be delayed...'

'Go on, Brewer, don't stop.'

Eyes closed, stupid expression on the little shit's face. 'One Paddy turns to the other... says... Fook, last one goes...'

'Tell me!'

'We'll be up here...'

Spit dribbling from the corner of his mouth...

'...all night. '

'What did he say?'

'Fook. '

'Say it again, Brewer.'

'...Fook.'

The Brewer breathing fast and shallow now, lips turning blue. Then a spasm...

The first.

Ross watching him die, listening to the trains going by, the weird violin music still playing on the CD, Laurie something-or-other, maybe she was a short jock, name like 'Laurie'. Thinking, Death always was instantaneous, it was just the time it took to get to that point that varied... that moment between one heart beat and the one that didn't follow.

Waiting as long as he could stand.

Making sure.

Then Ross re-sealed the cellophane pack, put it in the inside pocket of his raincoat, and let himself out of the flat.

Hot shot.

Watch him burn.

That's how Ross would have off'd the fucker.

Denise uneasy about the call.

'Giles there?'

Not recognising the voice. Male.

'No, he's at work.'

Telephone salesman? They usually rang at dinner time, just when you had sat down to eat, knowing it was the best time to find people in.

'Who is this I'm speaking to?'

'I'm Giles's wife.'

Not saying her name.

'Denise?'

Denise hoping she was not committing a *faux pas*.

Trying to place the voice.

'I was wondering if you would give Giles a message for me?'

'I'm sorry, who is this?'

'No matter, I'm ringing for Harry.'

Harry? Did they know a Harry?

'You don't know Harry and neither does Giles.'

'I don't understand.'

'Giles will.'

The Magazine.

Something Giles had written?

Losing patience.

'This Harry you're ringing for... you said something about a message?'

'Most certainly.'

Confusion becoming curiosity, the voice music hall camp, like that actor in *Are You Being Served?*.

'And?'

'And?' Mimicking her voice, 'Don't you go getting on your high horse with me, Denise.'

Curiosity replaced with...

Not fear...

Not anger.

Annoyance.

'Please don't make me appear rude by having to put the phone down on you.'

'Tell Giles...'

'Tell Giles what?'

'Celeste sends her regards.'

'Celeste?'

'Harry's wife.'

'I'm sorry, you've completely lost me.'

'Ask Giles.'

Falling in.

Celeste! The woman Giles had been seeing, 'We'll talk about it later, work something out,' Giles saying over the phone this morning.

Hearing Jane beep from the road outside, car doors slamming, Mandy and Kate's high-pitched voices coming closer to the front door, one of them falling into it with a crash.

Jane's voice, 'Kate, stop that!'

Denise thinking, God, is it that time, already?

A click and the line went dead.

Chapter 4
She swallowed the bird,
To catch the spider...

Ross didn't know what he must have been thinking of, coming this way, down Fulham Palace Road, always chock-a-block, especially between Lillie Road and The Broadway, whatever time of day it was. Idling in the inside lane, stuck behind a number 11 bus, people on the platform wondering if it was going to be quicker to walk – what was it about number 11 bus drivers, crazy fuckers, every one of them? You saw them sometimes, treated Hammersmith Broadway like a skid patch. Rush hour in full swing, traffic easing slowly towards The Broadway, Ross gaining ground on the traffic in the outside lane, didn't they know anything, those stupid bastards, traffic bound to move faster in the inside lane with a left-hand filter up ahead? Maroon Renault cutting between Ross and the bus, just worked it out for himself, Ross leaving him the space. No sense busting a gut in London traffic. All you ended up with was a coronary, just look at the state of most London cabbies – completely fucking mental.

Level with the front of the Hammersmith Odeon now, beneath the flyover, the number 11 forcing its way out into the traffic going round The Broadway, taking it slow, but not about to stop for anybody... 'They all got fucking brakes, haven't they?' Harry would say that when he thought Ross was driving too politely. Maybe that's what Harry needed, a number 11 bus driver as his fucking chauffeur.

On the pavement outside the Odeon, crowd of kids in leather jackets, long hair, all milling around, heavy duty motorbikes lining the curb, posters on the front of the building, around the entrance, reading: *Heavy Metal Week*, bands Ross had never heard of: Motorhead, Saxon, Girlschool. The Brewer hadn't been too far out when he's taken the piss out of Ross's taste in music. *Danny Boy*. So what was so wrong about liking a song like *Danny Boy*? It certainly beat the shit out of most of the crap you heard on the radio nowadays. Ross could remember Mary crying when she heard *I'll Take You Home Again, Kathleen* – Joseph Locke – crying because her name was Mary and not Kathleen, because she would never be able to imagine he was singing it just for her.

When Ross was a kid nobody even had a record player. There was one uncle used to buy sheet music whenever he went into Tralee, had to wait till he was pissed before he would bash out a tune on the piano at family get-togethers, making a fucking racket all night long... then thinking of his Aunt Rôsin how she used to sing *Moorlough Shore*, her husband, Sean, accompanying her on the fiddle...

Different fucking world.

A lifetime away.

Watching the kids outside the Odeon, an old lady threading her way through the crowd, shoulders swaying from side to side with the weight of the shopping, she probably walked like that when she *wasn't* carrying shopping, rolling gait, she'd been doing it so long, home in time to get the old man's dinner started, him sat there in front of the afternoon racing, never dreamt of lifting a finger.

Thought of Mary, again, how right from the start he had sworn that it wasn't going to be like that with them, her becoming his workhorse, losing her figure, the light slowly going out in her eyes... like with his Mammy, in her grave before sixty. Easing out behind the bus, a young girl leaning against the safety barrier catching his eye. Sixteen, maybe? Ross found it harder to tell as he got older. Staring out across the traffic towards the station entrance in the middle of The Broadway, waiting for someone? A boyfriend, meeting up to buy concert tickets? White T-shirt, could do with a wash – and in this weather! Tight jeans, nothing special, except she had caught Ross's eye as he was pulling out into the traffic. Found himself imagining the shape of her boobs beneath the T-shirt, surprising himself – Christ! I'm starting to think like Harry – then wondering what it would be like, another woman, not Mary, not the girl either, what the fuck, he was no cradle-snatcher... seeing the red Corsair just in time, braking and cutting to the left...

Fucking *prat*!

Not even noticing the kid on the motorcycle, coming up on the inside, heading for the same gap.

'One thing… now I'll discover how many people were the friends of the editor of *London Live!*, and how many are the friends of Chris Warren.'

'You know where I stand on that, don't you, Chris'

'Goes without saying, Giles.'

But Giles wasn't sure how he meant that. Chris always was a sarcastic bastard, could never open his mouth without it sounded like he was taking the piss. Chris, while speaking, extending his arm, impeding the progress of the waitress to another table, holding the bottle of Sancerre, their second, now saying: 'Would you bring us another, love, one that's been in the cooler longer than five minutes.'

The waitress, already laden with a full tray of drinks, took the bottle, added it to the tray.

'If looks could kill.'

'Fucking antipodeans.'

Giles saying, 'She's New Zealand. Didn't you hear, when we ordered the bottle, she said *sincere*, like they watch *tillyvision* and not television.'

'Antipodean, Giles, means diametrically opposite – applies to New Zealanders just as much as Australians. How the fuck are you going to get by without me as your editor, eh?'

Giles draining his glass.

Chris saying, 'Anyway, here's to the next bottle of *sincere*, when the stupid bitch finally manages to find us a cold one.'

Chris had been drinking since eleven-thirty.

The hospitality bar in his office, a few pints at lunchtime, 'Glass of wine in Flaubert's when they open?' Standing at Giles's desk, the usual florid smile, meaning, 'Fancy making a night of it?' Only, Giles was going home. He had promised Denise… things would change.

'You should have read the signs, Chris.'

'Like when he announced his daughter's birth in *The Times*?'

'Hauled Nadia over the coals for writing up that restaurant in Kentish Town, offered a reasonable three course meal for under a tenner.'

'"What the fuck do you think this is all about, Nadia? Do

you really think we are catering for a readership that's looking for a meal out for under a tenner?" Tears, the poor woman was in tears.'

Giles playing the game.

'"Sympathetic, our readership may be – but do they really want their noses rubbed in the plight of psychotic winos, the problems OAPs have with their heating bills, and why the fuck so many black drug dealers get their arses kicked in police custody? Do they really, really, *really* want it rammed down their throats every sodding week!"'

'Our Graeme, eh?'

Both laughing as the waitress arrived with a new bottle. Chris pouring the wine, saying, 'Fucking cunt!'

Both drinking in silence for a while, then Giles saying, 'Your contract's okay, you won't be out for a bob or two?'

'If only.'

'Oh?'

'Oh, indeed. Graeme has been stalling for three months on the renewal, "In the pipeline, Chris, you know what they say, can't hurry a solicitor…" all the usual shit.'

'Unfair dismissal?'

'He offered severance.'

'And?'

'And I took it… Elaine screaming blue fucking murder every first of the month, Natasha needs this, Natasha needs that, what else could I bloody do? Besides, I want another job in this town, the last thing I need is a reputation for being difficult.'

Chris, difficult?

Giles amused, but keeping it to himself, saying: 'Word gets round, you'll be able to pick and chose. Six months from now and you'll be thanking Graeme for doing you a favour.'

'I wish I had your confidence.'

Filling Giles's glass to the brim, looking around for the waitress, catching her eye, Giles wanting to say, 'For God's sake please don't click your fingers.'

Chris clicking his fingers, saying to Giles, 'I blame that fucking slag from Television Centre.'

'Helen?'

'Well, who else?'

Giles remembering the last time Helen Monkton had been at

the office, just before she and Graeme had gone off to Mauritius, Chris saying, 'Helen, how nice. We so rarely have the pleasure.' Or, another time, in Graeme's office, 'And how's Helen keeping these days? Do give her my regards, won't you?'

Two-faced bastard!

'Here's to Helen, face like a Monkfish.'

'That's hardly fair, Chris.'

'No really, just think about it... has Graeme gone completely ga-ga, or what?'

The waitress at their table.

Chris ignoring her, saying, 'Oxygen deprivation, that's what it is. Spends too much time with his head stuffed between her fucking thighs... it's official, Graeme Tate is no longer of this planet.' Then, to the waitress, 'I don't suppose you have a half way decent Armagnac?'

Giles checking his watch.

Seven-fifteen.

Oh, shit!

'Chris, I'd love to, but...'

'Nonsense, tonight of all nights.'

'We have Remy, sir.'

Pronounced 'Rimmy', as in 'Jimmy'.

'*Rimmy*?' Chris saying, looking at Giles, laughing. 'Could be our luck's in, here, if you like that sort of thing,' then, to the waitress, 'Remy,' accentuating the accent... 'Remy Martin is a brandy. It is not an Armagnac.'

To Giles: 'Fucking colonials.'

Giles wanting to push back his chair, get up, walk out... down Old Compton Street to Leicester Square, thirty minutes on the train, he could be home...

The waitress waiting.

Impassive.

'How about a Calva, love?'

'Calva?'

Hair, pale yellow, flaxen, cropped short. Sleepy blue eyes giving away nothing, just waiting for this to be over. Echoing Chris's pronunciation, exactly.

'Calvados, love... it's an apple brandy, comes from Normandy, that's in France.'

Right now, just get up, walk away.

'Only *Rimmy*, sir.'

'Yeah Gods!'

Giles offering the waitress a conciliatory smile, which she ignored.

'So be it,' Chris said. 'Two *Rimmy's*, large ones, and make it this side of Christmas, if you please.'

Giles thinking:

Better ring Denise.

After the Remy.

Ray was sure that this time, tonight, it was going to be all right, no problem. Just thinking about that woman was enough. 'Is that all? Aren't you going to do anything?' Not sobbing any more, just angry. Ray wouldn't have been at all surprised if she hadn't started stamping her foot, she was that angry. Her standing there starkers, now that would have been a laugh. Then, her saying, 'You dirty little bastard. Is that all you're worth?'

Her brat crying now. Frightened by her Mum's anger. She shouldn't have gone off on one like that...

Spoiling it.

Making the kid cry.

Ray steering the Honda with his knees, the bike leaning one way, Ray's shoulders, the other, steering the way the motorcycle cops did at those exhibitions his mum and dad used to take him to see at Earls Court when he was a kid. Fucking boring, except for the motorcycle cops: weaving between the cones, formation riding... Triumph Thunderbirds, then finishing up with the pyramid, six abreast, the cops all piled up on each others shoulders, flash bastards. Least it used to keep them occupied, not out on the road nicking people.

Traffic hardly moving, Ray pretending he was one of those motorcycle cops, weaving in and out between the slow-moving cars, holding second, inside or outside lane, depending on which fucker was holding him up, pissed off that he had caught the rush hour. His old man saying, when he had come in, had a bath, changed his clothes, 'Wonders will never cease.' Sarcastic sod. And then, 'Find time to sit with your mother for a bit, Ray, she's not at her best today.' His mother calling from upstairs, from the bedroom, that pathetic voice she always put on when she wanted her own way, 'Ray, is that you, Ray?' Christ, he hated the smell of that room, her lying there propped up on her pillows, face all waxy and gaunt, like a ghost, already, 'Blessed relief, it will be, you can't imagine, Ray, you just can't imagine the pain, nobody knows.' Ray remembering she always used to say things like that, even before she was ill. Shouting up the stairs, 'Can't stop, Ma, meeting Susanne.' Getting his helmet back on before he could hear her reply, but still hearing the old man, beside him at the front door, saying, 'It's not going to be long now, Ray, you know that.'

Ray now thinking the same thing.

But not about his mother.

About him and Susanne.

She would be home by now, always got in from work just after six. Monday night, dinner left warm in the oven, Bette would be off to her Spanish dance club with that prat, Ted, her dance partner. No prizes for guessing what he was really after, dirty old fucker. Jim would be having a quick one at The Stag then off to his weekly card school with his mates, whoever's house it was this week, throwing good money after bad. Pontoon, three card brag, finishing off with a round of nine card...

Once Ray had become a bit of a fixture, Jim had invited him along one night, cost him a fucking fortune, that on top of the whip-round for booze and crisps. Still, they were all right, Jim and Bette. A right laugh. Ray couldn't get used to that... parents that were a right laugh, not after what he'd had to put up with at home ever since he could fucking walk.

Braking hard.

Geezer on foot, skinhead, from out of nowhere, behind a van going the other way. T-shirt – this weather! – showing off his tattoos, ankle-swingers, DMs, right there in front of him, could have got himself killed, Ray too, the stupid fucker. Giving each other the look, there in the middle of the Fulham Road, Ray about to shout, not even getting to what he would shout, clocking the skin's expression, giving the machine a rev, clutch out, while the skin cut between two cars, made it to the other pavement, still looking back, just asking for Ray to come out with something.

Just like the woman.

Asking for it.

Ray telling himself...

Any other time, you tosser.

But not tonight.

Not with the house to themselves till ten-thirty. Bette would be back then, making a cup of tea for dance partner Ted – Christ, what an old fart he was, like home from home it was, with him around. 'When are you going to make something of yourself, son? By your age I'd done two years in the army, served my country. Do you some good, that would, two years in the army.' Sipping his tea, drop of milk, two sugars, always had to have a cup with a saucer. Two chocolate-backed digestives to go with it. Doorman all his life, commissionaire he called it, right up to when he retired, New Zealand House, up the west end near Trafalgar Square, that was the last place he worked. Outside all weather, peaked hat and uniform with brass buttons, going 'Yes, sir, no sir,' all day long, arsehole crawling. What made him think he was so fucking superior?

Gave him the right?

Full of airs and graces.

Like the woman.

Still wanting the last word.

'My husband is twice the man you'll ever be.'

Ray thinking: 'We'll see about that...'

Tonight.

With Susanne.

'A decent haircut wouldn't go amiss, either, son. It pays to look presentable in this world.'

Passing shot, Bette helping him on with his coat, gabardine three-quarter length with a green corduroy collar, like all the old geezers wore trotting round the shops behind the missus.

Silly fucker.

What did he know?

Doing up his scarf, finding his trilby, Bette escorting him to the front door. Jim, in by now, tucking into something on toast with a cup of instant before going up to bed, 'Not my night, Ray. Cards just not falling right for me.' Bette and Ted on the doorstep, letting out all the heat, discussing how they were a dead cert to win the regional qualifiers – why Jim put up with it, fuck only knows. Ray, he would have kicked the fat fucker's backside all down the street…

Seeing the dickhead on the racing bike up ahead. Claude Butler frame, more gears then sense, drop bars. The kind of bike Ray would have loved to have had as a kid. 'You can just get that nonsense right out of your head.' Or, 'You think I've got nothing better to do than worry about you all day long?' And the clincher, 'Sometimes, I think you think money grows on trees.' The old man chipping in, 'You know how nervous your mother is, son, don't make her more upset.' Ray's revenge, what seemed like years later, showing them the motorbike parked out in the road. The old man saying, 'Where did the money come from, that's what I'd like to know.' 250 Suzuki, before Ray passed his test, part-exchanged for the CBR 600.

Coming up behind the racer, geezer dressed for the part, luminous yellow cross-straps, one of those stress-plastic helmets looked like a walnut, red reflector pads on his elbows, standing on the pedals, fucking oblivious, with Walkman headphones glued to his ears…

Ray, right behind him, leaning on the horn.

Couldn't hear a fucking thing.

All around, geezers dressed for the office, thinking about what's for dinner, sealed in their motors, used to this ritual every fucking day. Sat there in the traffic, tapping their fingers on the steering wheel, all tapping the same rhythm, listening to some crap on Capital Radio, waiting for the next traffic update, breakdowns, accidents – bomb alerts, even, fucking IRA – hoping they should be so lucky it wasn't their neck of the woods. Stroll on! The cyclist ahead cutting suddenly into the inside lane leaving Ray room to open the throttle, still holding second, give it some *at last*.

Straight down the central white, passing a double-decker, windows all steamed up, just missing an old granny with her shopping on a crossing, then under Hammersmith Flyover, out into The Broadway… no, she shouldn't have said that, that woman. Shouldn't have looked at him that way. Supercilious bitch… leaning the bike, grounding the exhaust, sparks flying. Big American job right in front of him – no, fuck, it was a Roller – leaning some more to take him on the passenger side, finding the gap. The Roller cutting to the left, Ray now in third, throttle wide open, surprised a motor that big could move so fast, the gap vanishing to nothing…

Shit!

Ray knowing he had to hit the brakes hard enough to lose it. The CBR sliding sideways, burning rubber, more sparks as he grounded it, engine screaming, the back wheel with no bite on the road, thank Christ for the fucking crash bars, staring at the road six inches from his face, grateful that it had stopped moving. Cars pulling up all around, wheels losing their grip on the wet surface… but not the Roller. Fucker hadn't even seen him.

Drivers leaning on their horns further back, couldn't see what the hold-up was all about. Ray lying in the road, waiting for the pain, knowing he must have broken something, afraid to look down at his legs, see a bone poking through, blood all over the place… amazed when the pain didn't come.

'You all right, son?'

Son? Why was he everybody's fucking son?

Ray pulling himself from under the bike, standing up, trying to stop his legs shaking, but couldn't help it.

Another voice:

'Silly bugger. Did you see the speed he was doing?'

Picking the CBR up, not easy, the fucking weight of it. Fairing all dented along one side, paint scratched to buggery, big graunch in the exhaust… fuck it!

'You should sit down for a bit, son. Get that helmet off, loosen your collar.'

Ray astride the bike, now. Pressing the starter. Once, twice… oh, shit, no! Then the machine roaring into life. Big crowd of heavy metal geezers out front of The Odeon, all pressed up against the safety barrier watching the show, giving a big cheer as the bike started up. Tears of rage in Ray's eyes, hidden beneath his visor.

The first motorist saying, again: 'You all right, son?'

Course he was fucking all right!

Denise sighing.

'Because it's not very terribly well written, that's why. And besides, all that chopping off of heads, it strikes me that Jack wasn't a particularly nice person.'

Not her Jack – Denise's Jack in Dyfed…

Jack the Giant Killer.

Explaining to Mandy why she didn't want to read her the story.

'But the giants are all ugly.'

'That's still no reason to go chopping their heads off… bathroom! And don't forget your teeth, brush them properly. I'll be up for an inspection in a minute.'

'Oh, Mum!'

'There's no "Oh, Mum" about it.'

Eight o'clock.

Sod you, Giles.

How could you do this?

Mandy still standing there.

'Bed!'

Wondering if she should have phoned him at the Magazine, after the phone call, told him about it. Listening while Mandy, upstairs, washed and got undressed, shouting up the stairs, 'I'll be up in five minutes to turn the light out.'

Worried.

Surely, after their phone conversation this morning, how had Giles put it? 'We'll have a long chat tonight, over dinner… work something out.' After his protestations, 'This time it will be different,' not even Giles would do this to her… perhaps there was something wrong, something to do with that man on the telephone, 'Tell Giles, Celeste sends her regards.' That camp, creepy voice… a message from Harry? Celeste's husband?

Turning off the oven, the garlic bread, on low since six-thirty, burnt to a crisp. Picking at the salad on the table, eating a slice of salami, *Milano*, Giles's favourite – why on earth had she bothered? Pouring herself another glass of red wine, surprised to find the bottle now empty. When had she opened it? Just after Jane had brought Mandy home, at four-thirty.

'Is he still here?'

'Is who still here?'

'The surveyor, darling, you told me he was coming this afternoon.' Caught out in a silly lie. Jane hovering on the doorstep, waiting to be invited in, 'Don't tell me he didn't turn up?'

'Oh, yes,' Denise saying, 'the surveyor, yes he did come. He's been gone about half an hour.'

'Did it go all right?'

'Yes, perfectly.'

'Well…'

'Tomorrow… usual time?'

Unable to resist it, pleased with herself that she had been able to say that to Jane, Jane giving Denise one of her old fashioned looks, still waiting for the invitation. Denise fighting the easy option, not saying, 'Just a quick coffee, then,' a small battle won… leaving Denise free to get on with the dinner, Mandy watching children's television before the call, before that creepy man saying, 'Don't you go getting on your high horse with me…'

Looking at the wall clock again.

Oh, Giles!

Please don't do this to me…

Opening another bottle of red wine, putting the bottle on the kitchen table, next to her glass, then going upstairs, Mandy fast asleep already, tucking her in, turning out the light, feeling the emptiness of the house…

Hearing the phone ringing, downstairs.

Hoping it would be Giles.

Even if it meant listening to another of his bloody excuses.

'It's an important vote… Chris is insisting that I hang on here for the result, otherwise we'll miss this issue.'

'…his statement changes the whole picture… I'm going to have to do a complete rewrite.'

'Swindon of all bloody places… animal rights lunatics on the rampage again… fuck knows what time I'll get home.'

Or…

The old chestnut.

'It's Chris, he's still feeling very down about Elaine… said I'd go for a drink with him.'

Taking the stairs two at a time.

Counting the rings.

It was Barbara.

'You sound a bit breathless, am I interrupting something?'

Denise saying, 'Not unless I've taken to practicing self-abuse.'

Denise surprised at herself, saying something like that, even to Barbara.

Barbara laughing, 'Abuse? That's not the word I would use

– you ought to try it sometime, you might find it a lot more satisfying than that bloody husband of yours.' Then, 'Giles out on the tiles as usual, then?'

'He's due back any moment, actually.'

'Isn't he always!'

'Barbara…' resisting the urge to defend Giles, knowing, in doing so, she was only defending herself.

'Have I caught you at a bad time?'

'No… no, actually, I was going to ring you today, earlier.'

'Bloody glad you didn't, I've been up to my ears in it.'

Barbara… *Always* up to her ears in it.

'Just put a job on the train for Allan,' – her agent in London – 'book cover for Bantam, wanted yesterday, as per bloody usual.'

Denise not wanting to explain to Barbara that she and Giles were having problems, Barbara, 'Giles! Why you ever married him, I don't know,' always so absolute, so judgmental, 'One day you'll surprise me by saying you and Giles *don't* have a problem,' no, not wanting to go through all that with her. Anxious that Giles might be trying to ring…

The line engaged.

Saying, 'It was just for a chat, that's all. With half term coming up, I was thinking it might be nice to come down for a couple of days, with Mandy.'

'All summer, I've been asking you to come down, and you have to wait till November. I have to warn you, the weather is a pile of shit. It's been chucking it down for days.'

'Still, it would be a break.'

'No Giles?'

'You know Giles, he's always too busy to get away anywhere.'

Remembering the last time Giles had gone down to Wales with them, four years ago, was it that long? A New Year's Eve, Barbara still with John, sharing the big farmhouse with that other couple they moved down from Kew with… Alice and Roger. Giles hating every minute of it, 'Failed sociologist turned market gardener,' talking about Roger, 'who does he think he's kidding with all that back to the soil bollocks?'

Two films on the television, that's the kind of New Year's Eve it was, they had watched both of them… *Calamity Jane* and *Klute*, Giles, perverse, arguing that *Klute* was a more sexist film than *Calamity Jane*, 'So, she's a prostitute, at least she had her independence, then she agrees to marry the copper, be his little woman – what a cop-out.' And then Alice coming out with, 'Romantic love is the greatest threat to womankind,' Giles quoting her to Denise two years later when they heard from Barbara that Alice had run off with an Algerian who rented a caravan at the bottom of their field, left Roger, her two small boys...

All for what.

Denise had wondered if there was something she was missing.

What kind of passion could inspire that?

To desert your children?

Giles saying: 'I'm going to have a T-shirt printed... Earnestness Kills!' And: 'God preserve us from bloody minded vegetarians.'

Denise saying, now, 'Of course, if you're busy, yourself?'

'Don't be daft. I'd love to see you – and Mandy.'

Jack's name hanging in the air, Denise wanting to ask Barbara how he was, whether he had taken up with anybody, it was a bit like musical chairs down there, you didn't know who was living with who from one minute to the other... realising she was thinking like Giles. 'Life swap? Wife swap, more like it!'... was how Giles would have put it.

Barbara saying, 'Come as soon as you like. It doesn't have to be half term. I've never seen a child, yet, suffered from missing a few days of school.'

Denise, half turning to see the wall clock.

Eight-thirty-five.

'Look, I have to go, Barbara, something in the oven.'

'Wouldn't do for Giles's dinner to spoil, would it?'

'Barbara... look I'll give you a call next week, about coming down.'

'Just make sure you do.'

'Speak soon.'

'Sure.'

The phone back in it's cradle.

Denise expecting it to ring again, immediately.

Thinking, why don't phones look like phones any more?

All numbers.

In the handset.

No dialling.
Giles…
You bastard!
Ring.

Ross was at the junction of Shepherds Bush Road and Brook Green, intersection of the rat run that avoided Hammersmith Broadway, brought you out at Olympia, waiting on the red, thinking about The Brewer, how such a prat-fall could ever have existed in the first place. If there was a God, like fuck did he look out for drunks and fools. Still in drive, feeling the pull of the transmission, the torque of the six-point-five-litre engine held in check by Ross's right foot on the brake pedal. How long was it going to take, this fucking traffic. Get across to North London, drop off Harry's motor. In the rear view mirror, noticing the kid on the motorcycle, coming up on the outside. One of those Japanese jobs, all you ever saw on the road these days… respecting the lines, the performance, but not, still, thinking of them as the real thing, despite how could he forget that first time they took first five places at The Isle of Man… when was it, early seventies?

Too clean.

No leaking oil.

Not even a kick-start…

Break your leg, the timing was out of sync.

Thinking of the greats – Norton SS, Triumph Bonneville, 350 Gold Star, BSA… the 'Goldie', now *that* was Ross's idea of a real motorbike. That smell of scorched vegetable oil hanging above the surface of the road, the exhaust baffling, like the roar of a Thor Missile lifting off from the launch pad when you wound it down from top to second at eighty, showed the fuckers what you had in reserve. Who needed to check what was coming up behind?

Kid had no idea what he was missing.

Watching him now in the offside wing mirror. Noticing the dents in the fairing, paintwork scratched to fuck – kid must have dropped it – coming up past the Roller on the outside…

Thinking of the winding, early morning road down from

Cahersiven to Waterville, Ballinskelligs Bay, the Kerry Ring Road, like a circus now, all summer, fucking tourists, again... the Goldie, rebore finished the day before, new cylinders arrived from Cork in the morning. English shit, big house out at Killorglin, wore one of those leather flying helmets, goggles, talked about opening a restaurant in Kenmare, work for a living, on the phone, expecting favours because everybody knew he was who he was... Hanging on to the machine, first, because, what else could he do? Saying, over the phone, 'Just as soon as we get the new rings,' but then, the job finished, taking the bike out, shaving off the minutes to Waterville and back, running it in. Then, that last morning, giving it everything, the bike talking back...

Saying: Fuck you.

It's not me got something to prove.

Seventeen.

You had to be that young...

To hear a motorcycle talk.

Doing what he swore he would never do, working in the old man's garage, two miles up the road from Cahersiven, one pump, workshop, fixed up tractors for the most part – post war production turning them out by the thousand, even down there, they had them – fourteen when he left school, fuck you and good riddance to the nuns...

Now what?

The man from the North.

That was what.

Six weeks he was there. How long was that when you were seventeen? Ross in the parlour, supposed to sleep on one of those chairs, back went down, okay, if you were a midget. Remains of the fire, big warm glow, but, how come some stranger got his bedroom, first crack at anything going on the dinner table, two eggs for breakfast? Guilty now, but glad then, when The Garda kicked in the door, four-thirty one morning, automatic weapons, no fucking nonsense...

Ross's old man, seven years, a life sentence. Two years into his time, one year almost to the day after Ross held his mother tight, said goodbye to his three brothers, his two younger sisters, crossed the water looking for work, money to send home...

Heart attack.

That's what the priest who came to call told his mother.

Waiting on the green…

As the kid manoeuvred his motorcycle in front of the Roller, hoisted the bike on to its stand, dismounted, took a hammer – looked like a fifteen-pounder – out of the side-pannier.

What the fuck…?!

The kid leaning across the bonnet like he was about to clean the windscreen, swinging the hammer, the glass shattering, frosting over. Then appearing at the nearside passenger window, casual as you like, heaving the hammer at the two side windows, then the back window, the glass hanging there, sagging, held in place by the filaments of the rear window heater, approaching along the driver's side, now…

Rear window behind Ross.

Still taking his time.

Afterwards, Ross thought the kid might have been whistling…

But not sure he hadn't imagined it.

Ross knowing what *should* happen next. Seeing the kid as dead, already. Go into reverse, open the driver's door wide, foot down, knock the fucker into next week…

Or, better still:

Transmission in neutral, release the safety belt, open the door, blocking the kid's path. Don't get out, that way the kid can't get in a good swing with the hammer. Grab the fucker by the jacket, pull down hard, hear his teeth connect with the door sill, then straight arm him in the balls, leave the fucker lying there in the road.

Select drive.

Steamroller that Japanese heap of shit that was blocking his path.

The kid smashed the last window.

Shards all over Ross's lap, the safety glass turning into hard-edged confetti, Ross thinking… twenty-eight gramme bag, cellophane wrapped, pure white, less the amount The Brewer had shot up to top himself, lying there underneath his raincoat on the front seat. The Filth leaning in the window, saying, 'Hello, Ross, long time no see. Charley about, is he?'

You went down once, could be bad luck.

Twice, you were a fucking idiot.

Ross punched a hole in the frosted windscreen, saw the kid

putting the hammer away in the pannier, took out his Parker
and notebook from his inside jacket pocket – companion set,
leather bound notebook, present from Mary last Christmas, she
was amazed he hadn't lost it yet, left it lying around someplace
– wrote down the kid's registration number, noting for the first
time the make of the bike, Honda CBR 600, the kid starting it
up, driving away on the green.

Put the notebook and pen back in his inside pocket.

The lights now back to amber.

Saw, in his wing mirror, a motorist, two cars back, out of his
car, walking forward. Put the Roller in drive as the lights
changed to red, jumped the lights, turning hard right into
Brook Green Road, pushing up to sixty on the clock, between
the Victorian terraced houses, the green, and the tennis courts
on his right, woman with a pram pulling back, screaming at
him, thinking, Christ, that would have *really* fucked it...

Wondering about the kid.

Why he'd done it.

Jesus! Harry was going to go bananas when he saw the state
of the motor.

When he was a kid, still at primary school, Giles used
to hold his breath till he passed out. He didn't want
to die. He wanted attention. That's what the family
doctor had told his mother, when she'd taken him round the
surgery: 'The boy is looking for attention.'

'Attention? I wait on him hand and foot now, as it is.'

'He lacks security.'

'I hope you're not trying to tell me I'm not a good mother.'

Both of them avoiding bringing it up – that Giles's dad had
run off with a secretary from the insurance office where he
worked, neither of them had been seen since, two years back,
now, when Giles was six.

'Not at all, Mrs Barton. Under the circumstances...

The doctor offering to refer Giles to the psychiatric department of Ducane Road Hospital, but Giles's mother having none
of it.

The neighbours, already with enough to talk about.

Giles wished he could do that now. Hold his breath till he passed out, anything... rather than have to sit here any longer, Chris wallowing in self-pity, slagging off Graeme, Helen Monkton, his ex-wife, Elaine – blaming everybody except himself. Giles remembering taking a deep breath, holding it, cheeks ballooning, face going red, eyes tight shut. The ringing in his ears, his mother screaming in his face, 'Giles! You stop that nonsense right this minute, you hear me!' The dizziness coming, the black waves...

For attention?

The last thing he needed right now was attention... everybody in the wine bar aware that Chris was making a right pain in the arse of himself. The New Zealand waitress gone with the last of the after-work crowd; the waiter, taken over her station, a young bloke with a quiff he kept combing, black T-shirt tucked into French designer jeans, moved like a dancer, probably was a dancer. The tables he was serving, mostly couples, in for a quiet drink after a meal or an early film, all aware of the two pissheads, one of them talking too loud, did he really think what he had to say was of any conceivable importance to the rest of the room?

Giles just sober enough to realise this, watching Chris's lips moving, no longer hearing what he was saying, realising, Oh Christ, he detested this man, always had... this man who, as of this morning, was no longer his boss, could no longer have any effect on Giles's life, whatsoever – so, why was he still bothering to put up with all this shit? Saying, 'While we're on the subject of home truths...' Aware of the stages, of which stage he had now reached, Denise saying to him, once, 'I don't think you quite realise just how boring you are when you're drunk, Giles.' 'Garrulous pontification,' that's how she described it. And that next stage... an irrepressible desire to shock.

Looking for attention?

Still?

Giles's father had been in touch shortly after he and Denise were married. Rang from Dublin, where he was living with the other woman. Told Giles he and Moira had married, got three kids of their own, that they were very happy. Why didn't Giles and Denise come over for a holiday sometime, Giles could meet his half-brother and two half-sisters? The first contact in all those years, Giles's mother in the ground six months.

Ovarian cancer... the size of a football before she had finally plucked up enough courage to go round to the doctor's about it.

Moira.

After all those years...

The other woman had a name.

Saying, to his father, 'I'll have to think about it.'

Neither of them making any further contact.

Giles, now, realising he should ring Denise, they must have a phone here, somewhere; instead, saying to Chris, '...get it off my chest.'

How come it was no fun, any more, getting pissed?

The waiter studiously ignoring Chris, both of them, their glasses empty, Chris saying, 'Be my guest, Giles. About time you had the floor for a bit... you know what I'm like when I've had a few.'

Billy Holiday on the sound system.

In Flaubert's, Billy Holiday was *always* on the sound system.

'Good taste by the yard,' Chris had said, one night, calling over the manager, bald Italian, with heavy framed glasses, always wore a red velvet waistcoat, saying to him, 'Can't we have a break from this? Do we have to listen to Billy bloody Holiday every night?' The manager saying, 'You don't like Billy Holiday?' Chris saying, 'Like her? I love her! If you loved Billy Holiday half as much as I do, you would treat her with a little more respect.'

Saying, now, 'I'm all ears, mate.'

Mate?

What was it about people who called you mate?

Made you instantly distrust them?

'You and me, I mean... I'm trying to be honest. What's the point if we can't be honest with each other.'

'Honest?'

'Yes, honest.'

Chris looking towards the waiter, again, 'Is there any danger of getting another drink in this dump, or what. Always the same... a place gets popular, service goes down the drain.' Then, to Giles, 'I've always respected you for that, Giles...'

'Respected me for what?'

'Your honesty.'

'Bollocks!'

'No, really.'

'That's what I'm talking about, Chris.'

'What *are* you talking about, Giles?'

'Respect… *self*-respect.'

'Exactly!'

Exactly?

Exactly what?

Giles now realising just how drunk he was.

How drunk they both were.

And too drunk to care.

'Do nothing till you hear from me,

Pay no attention to what folks say…'

Chris, joining in with the song, getting the words wrong, singing, 'No other arms may hold the ghost of a chance…'

Not noticing.

Giles saying, 'Ghost of a thrill,' not 'chance.'

'And they never will.'

'Who gives a fuck?'

The reality striking Giles for the first time… there would be no Chris tomorrow at the Magazine, coming out of his office, Giles just arrived, still with a hangover, bloodshot eyes, Chris saying, like he always did when they'd been on a bender the night before, 'Close those eyes, will you, before you bleed to death.'

Read it in an American crime novel.

Thought it was funny.

Every time.

Giles saying, 'I always resented you, Chris.'

'Resented *me*, what on earth for?'

Rudeness presented as candour.

Part of Denise's treatise on Giles when he was drunk.

Like fuck!

Home truths.

'All those ideas.'

'What ideas?'

'Features… week in, week out… my ideas.'

'Your ideas?'

Chris looking round again for the waiter.

'Just where is this heading, Giles?'

'You taking the credit.'

'What the fuck are you on about?'

'With Graeme.'

Chris finally aware of what Giles was saying, when he added. 'Thank Christ he finally wised up.'

Billy Holiday on a different song, now.

'Hush! Don't explain.'

'I don't believe I'm hearing this.'

'Oh, come on.'

'I need another drink.'

Then: 'I don't remember you rushing into Graeme's office this morning, bailing me out on the Sloane Ranger piece.'

Giles needing another drink, too, wishing, now, that he hadn't started this... what was the point? After tonight, Chris would be out of his life. He wouldn't need to put up with Chris-bloody-Warren ever again. Chris saying, 'I'll give you this much, Giles... you know how to kick a fucker when he's down.'

'Self-pity will get you exactly nowhere.'

'Well, what an ungrateful bastard you turned out to be.'

Giles now ignoring Chris, focusing on the payphone, just inside the door, by the coat stand, counting the tables between himself and the phone, wondering if he was going to make it without making a fool of himself. Fuck! was he pissed. Chris saying, '...talking like an absolute prat!' Then, 'What the fuck, where's that bloody poofter of a waiter? Giles, same again, another Remy?'

Giles on his feet.

Chair almost toppling, but he managed to catch it. So far, so good.

Ring Denise.

Tell her he was leaving now.

She would understand.

Chris's farewell drink.

Never again.

No...

'Hush! Don't explain!'

Celeste.

'You've messed with some dame.'

Fucking bitch!

'Skip that – lipstick.'

Not Billy.

Not Denise.

'Don't explain!'
Celeste.

The credits were rolling. Wet grey rooftops, *Coronation Street*, Ray thinking, Christ what a bunch of boring old farts, just imagine, having to live up North. Remembering the song his mates sang when United came down to Stamford Bridge:

'I goes down't pub and drink ten pints,
Gets myself rare plastered,
Then I goes back home and beats the wife,
'Cause I'm a big fat Northern bastard…'

Susanne didn't like to miss the *Street*, no matter what. Knew the names of all the characters, talked about them like they were real people, daft bitch. Sat here with her now on the settee, arms round each other, up close, the only light coming from the TV, Jim's pride and joy, big twenty-one inch Sony… Ray a bit annoyed with her that she was wearing jeans, wasn't going to make it any easier, all that sodding around to get them off, he would have lost it again by then.

Denise saying, 'Don't they have many blacks up north?'

Ray saying, 'Fucking good job, you ask me.'

Susanne saying, 'What about Gail, then? Telling her mum it might not be Brian's.'

Ray not sure who Gail was, caring even less… still in a good mood, despite the bike needed some work done on it, get the fairing hammered out, might even need a new panel, that would set him back a few bob, which he didn't have… thinking about the look on the big geezer's face, fucking magic, Ray, calm as you like, strolling round the Roller swinging the hammer, glass all over the place, geezer scared shitless, teach him to use his fucking mirrors!

And earlier.

The woman.

'Please… please don't hurt the child.'

Not so fucking superior all of a sudden.

Susanne turning towards him… kissing each other, Ray with his tongue in Susanne's mouth, not sure what to do with it, tasting tobacco, the Silk Cut Susanne liked to smoke, 'Low tar, they're much healthier for you,' Ray not too sure about that, but sure it wasn't making her mouth taste any better. Hand on her leg, squeezing, Susanne rolling towards him, her leg now across his lap, hand inside his shirt, running her fingers across his stomach, along the line of the belt, then pulling the tongue from the belt-buckle, undoing the top of his jeans...

Ray thinking about the woman.

Standing there.

Susanne saying, 'Do you want to be down here, or shall we go upstairs?'

Adverts on the TV now.

Some stupid bitch washing kids' clothes.

'It's come up beautifully white... two o'clock in the morning it goes everywhere but in their mouth.'

Advert for Daz.

Then, new tartar-control Crest, girl with big teeth, Susanne pressing her face into his neck, her lips sucking, drawing blood to the surface. Ray wanting to tell her to stop, her hand now holding him, knowing what his old lady was going to say if she saw the love-bite. 'Don't you have any shame, your poor mother lying at home in her sick-bed, what will people think... it all comes back to me, you know that, don't you, you dirty little bugger?'

Susanne saying, 'Now everybody will know you're mine.' Her hand still holding him, moving, kissing his face. The announcer on the television saying, 'Tonight at nine on Thames...' Her hand still moving, Susanne, right up close to his ear, saying, 'Is this all right? Do you want me to go faster... or slower?'

Ray saying, 'Don't talk,' surprised, hearing himself groan, then not able to help himself... Susanne kissing him all over the face, little pecks, going, 'Ray, Ray, Ray.'

Ray sitting up.

Not like this!

It wasn't supposed to happen like this.

Saying, 'Christ, Susanne, the state of my jeans.'

Susanne hugging his shoulders from behind.

Nuzzled into his neck.

Laughing.

Not taking him seriously.

'That's not very romantic.'

'Romantic! You call this romantic?'

Then the telephone ringing in the hall, Susanne, making a face, saying, 'I better answer that,' getting up from the settee, going out into the hall, hearing her saying, 'Hello?'

Ray covering himself up, doing up his belt, tucking in his T-shirt, feeling a right mess but not knowing what he could do about it. On the TV now, *The Best of the Carry Ons*... Sid James, Hattie Jacques, the rest of them, all coming out with lines like, 'That's a funny way to punch a ticket,' and, '...Until this huge Burpa came up in front of me and he pulled it out – a great big, shining sword.' How the fuck did they get away with it?

Susanne calling from the hall, 'It's for you, Ray... your Dad.'

Ray thinking, What the fuck does he want, ringing me here? Going out into the hall, taking the phone from Susanne, Susanne saying, 'Just up in the bathroom, won't be a minute,' hearing his old man say, 'Ray? Sorry, son, but you'd better come home. It's your mother... she's just passed away.'

Ray thinking, Sodding good that'll look, fucking great love-bite at my own mother's funeral.

Celeste came awake knowing Harry wasn't in the bed beside her, checking the bedside clock, eleven-thirty, they'd gone to bed early, Harry still tired from the jet lag.

She could hear him on the phone, the small room across the hall, they still called it the library, Harry used it as his office. Heard the phone go down, Harry standing in the bedroom door, nothing but his boxer shorts, Celeste saying, 'Who was that?'

Harry saying, 'Giles.'

Adding: 'Pissed as a fucking newt.'

Celeste sitting up in the bed, about to turn on the bedside light, changed her mind, reached for the Dunhills instead. Said, 'Giles? You must be joking.'

'No joke, Celeste. Said he wanted to talk to you. I told him you were asleep.'

'I don't believe this.'

Chapter 5
She swallowed the spider,
To catch the fly...

Denise was happy, happier than she had been in a long while, despite the cold, despite the mud – thank God she had had the foresight to put on some Wellingtons and woollen socks – despite having just 'come on' minutes before they were due to leave for the park, walking all the way, not much point trying to find a parking space near Ravenscourt Park on bonfire night, hoping she would be able to hold out till they got back home, the park crowded, long queues at all the Portakabin loos, the thought of changing a tampon in one of them, heaven forbid!

The display started at last, rockets flying up into the sky beyond the picket fence holding back the crowd, cascades of colour, bombshells exploding, starbursts, like giant Portuguese Men O'War, their tentacles drifting down, Denise worried that something might not have burnt out properly before it reached the ground. Everybody going, 'Oooh!' and 'Aaah!' as the sky filled with colour, the navigation lights of a landing aircraft, way above the display, momentarily confusing, her head held back, neck starting to ache, laughing, Giles beside her with Mandy on his shoulders, Mandy waving a sparkler, Denise saying, 'Careful with that, Mandy, don't burn your Daddy.'

Giles swearing, last night, no matter what was going on at the Magazine, he would be home to take them to the display, 'Firework night! You know what a big kid I am, no way am I going to miss that!' And true to his word.

Giles swearing, just seven short days ago, 'That's it! That's really fucking it! You there with *my* daughter, only two years old, you're supposed to be looking after her? Spreading your legs for some fucking tepee dweller!' About something that had happened four years ago.

Denise wondering why she had told him... knowing why she had told him.

Because she had wanted him to hurt as much as she was hurting.

Another bottle of red wine finished, the salad and cold cuts still on the table, Denise going up to bed at one o'clock, hating Giles for not coming home, frightened – no – uneasy about the telephone call, the fey voice, still awake an hour later, hearing Giles arrive, arguing with the taxi driver out on the pavement, 'You must be mistaking me for a tourist, chum!' Having trouble getting his key in the latch, coming straight up the stairs to their bedroom, so drunk he could hardly stand, saying, 'Denise, I'm sorry… Chris…' Then, 'Graeme fired him.'

Denise sitting up in bed, shouting, 'I don't care about Chris, I don't care about you, do you understand, I just don't bloody care!'

Mandy standing behind Giles in the doorway, in her pyjamas, Denise saying, 'See now, what you've done?', getting up, pushing past Giles, picking up Mandy and taking her back to the bed with her, Giles saying, 'It wasn't me doing all the shouting.'

Denise saying, 'Just get out, Giles, right out of the bloody house, for all I care.'

Giles going into Mandy's room, falling on to her bed, then coming back again, 'Denise, please, we have to talk.'

'It's two-thirty in the morning, Giles, and you're drunk.'

'Please, Denise, I'll go downstairs, put some coffee on.'

Denise lying awake until Mandy was asleep, putting on her dressing gown, downstairs in the kitchen, Giles seated at the table, filling a cup for her, saying, 'I did try to get away, you know Chris, at the best of times…'

Denise saying, 'I don't care about Chris. Chris-bloody-Warren can step under a bus for all I bloody care.' Feeling guilty about saying that, just as soon as the words left her mouth, then saying, 'Somebody rang this evening, about that woman you've been seeing, Celeste.'

'Celeste?'

'Well, that's her isn't it, all these nights the last few weeks?'

Giles confused. '*Who* rang?'

'A friend of her husband's, at least, that's what I assumed.'

'Not her husband?'

'I told you – it wasn't her husband.'

'Why should they ring here?' Then, 'Was there a message?'

'From Celeste, you mean? Giles, you bastard!'

'That's not what I meant, Denise, and anyway, I told you, it's over.'

'But still living in hope, that much is very obvious.'

'Denise!'

'What is it about this woman, Giles, what is it that she's got that I haven't?' Then, 'Tell me, I would truly like to know.'

Giles looking down into his coffee, 'I don't think you would.'

'Do you find me ugly? Unattractive?'

'Denise, you know that isn't it.'

'What then? '

Giles playing with his spoon, coffee spilling from the saucer on to the table-top, 'Perhaps…'

Denise waiting.

Wanting to take the spoon from his hand.

Hurl it at his face.

Giles saying, 'If we hadn't got married so young had more experience first, with other people.'

'Meaning?'

'If you'd had more partners, yourself, instead of only me.'

Wanting to hurt him.

'This Celeste, she's so experienced, is she?'

'She's older; of course, she's more experienced.'

'Older? How much older?'

Giles with that stupid expression on his face.

'She says she's forty-two, but I don't believe her.'

'Forty-two!'

'And the rest.'

'You're sleeping with a forty-two-year-old woman?'

'No, I said, she's older than that.'

'You're telling me that you'd sooner sleep with a middle-aged woman than me? Thanks a lot, Giles.'

'Doesn't that tell you something?'

Hurt him as much as she was hurting.

'Anyway, what makes you so certain I haven't?'

Denise, now, staring up into the night sky, golden rain, floating in the darkness, a salvo of bombshells, thick smoke drifting across from beyond the picket fence, Mandy, on Giles's shoulders, screaming with delight, 'Look at that one, Mummy, wasn't it loud?' holding her hands to her ears.

Denise remembering Giles's expression.

The look on his face.

'What are you saying?'

'You heard me, Giles. Don't look so shocked.'

'You've been with another man? Screwed somebody else?'

'A bit different when the shoe's on the other foot, isn't it?'

Giles saying, 'I don't believe this.'

Then: 'Who?

'When?

'You fucking bitch!'

Denise saying, simply, 'You wouldn't know him, at least, I don't think so. You might have seen him once or twice at one of Barbara's parties.'

'Fucking Barbara – I knew she'd have something to do with this. Set you up for it, did she, just to get one over on me?'

'It wasn't like that at all, Giles.' But, thinking, That might not be true.

Remembering Barbara saying, 'According to Giles, we women don't even *enjoy* sex. That can't say a lot for Giles, if you ask me.' About a piece Giles had written last year, for the magazine, 'A Case For Sexual Repression?', the two of them laughing about it over the telephone, Barbara saying, 'Lurid stuff, wish they'd rung me to do the illustrations, only Giles's magazine wouldn't have been able to afford me.' The piece proposing that the male genetic imprint drove men towards promiscuity, created conflict within monogamous relationships, the woman, with a different natural agenda to have children, to provide a safe environment for her progeny, Giles being perverse, as usual, delighting in flying in the face of contemporary ideas, then concluding that the 'Swinging Sixties' had all been a big mistake, that, for the sake of society, it was necessary that men's instincts be curbed... repressed. Barbara laughing, saying, 'Really quite an impressive argument, only Giles lifted the whole piece, I read it in *The Observer*, almost word for word, couldn't have been more than six months ago.'

Giles crying.

Saying, 'Tell me about it. How did it happen?'

She *had* hurt him.

Differently.

A hurt she couldn't understand. Going round the table to him. 'Keep your whoring hands off me!'

Kissing him.

'…spreading your legs for some fucking tepee dweller.'

Giles responding.

Mandy asleep upstairs, the two of them making love in a way they never had before…

And last night, too, Denise still surprised at herself, at Giles, aware of her cycle, not willing to just use Giles, unhappy to even contemplate the idea – Barbara saying, 'You ought to try it sometime, you might find it more satisfying…' What did Barbara know? Giles seducing her, actually seducing her, not even like their first time, Giles hadn't tried to seduce her that first time, just followed up on a drunken assumption…

Now aware.

That he couldn't.

Take her for granted.

Not any more.

Staring up into the dark sky, the fireworks finished, hearing Giles, beside her, say, 'Fuck the queue, I'm going to get a drink before they close the bar… you want anything?'

Mandy standing between them, Denise saying, 'No, not for me,' Giles about to walk off, Mandy saying, 'I'll come with you,' meaning, 'You meant for me to come, anyway, otherwise you would have asked me what I wanted to drink.'

Giles taking Mandy's hand, leading her off through the crowd, saying to Denise, 'Don't move from this spot, otherwise we'll never find you again.'

Denise saying, 'But you'll miss the lighting of the bonfire.'

The forty-foot mountain of wooden debris, old mattresses, discarded furniture, now the focus of attention, usually piled up over the weeks, but this year, for the first time, brought in on the day on the back of council trucks, after hedgehog preservationists had objected, Denise had been reading all about it in *The Brentford & Chiswick*.

Silly creatures.

Hibernating in a bonfire stack.

Giles gesturing towards where they would be lighting the fire, saying, 'A few feet either way, not going to make a lot of difference, is it?'

Denise alone in the crowd.

So many people.

Hard to believe she hadn't seen anybody she knew.

The man, beside her, saying, 'Mrs Barton?'

Denise, five-four in her stocking feet, 'petit – not short,' Giles liked to say, still, this man, his voice vaguely familiar, reaching only to her shoulder. Expensive bomber jacket, brown leather with white fur-lined collar, red mohair scarf trailing tassels front and back, student fashion, despite the cold, black watch cap, hair noticeably short.

'Sorry?'

An actor, perhaps. His voice familiar from talk-overs, from adverts on the TV, so many of them lived round here, now.

Giles appearing through a crush of young kids, bangers and jumping jacks exploding beneath their feet, laughing; Denise thinking, Somebody was going to get hurt, they weren't more careful... Giles holding a plastic beaker shoulder high, not wanting to get jostled, spill his beer, saying, 'Mandy, is she back with you?'

The man gone as Denise placed his voice.

The phone call.

The friend of Celeste's husband.

Harry.

'Mandy!' she screamed.

Celeste had slammed out of the house about seven o'clock, taking the keys to the Merc, saying, 'I can't be around you when you're in this kind of mood, Harry.'

Harry had watched some TV, couple of drinks, gone to bed.

Now it was twelve-fifteen. He could hear Celeste moving around downstairs, the television on loud, one of those soft porn Hollywood films she was always hiring from Blockbuster, it was probably her coming home that had woken him up. Still, he was relieved. One of these days, amount she drunk, Celeste was going to wrap that Merc round a lamp post. He reached over to turn on the bedside light. Changed his mind.

Lay there in the dark, Tim still there in the room with him, from the dream, his voice, flat west London monotone, like it was only yesterday, coming into Harry's bedroom, the suite de Groot had sorted out for them at The Wilhelmina, Den Haag, Harry still pissed from the night before, 'You up for breakfast, or what?'

Harry saying, 'Sliced cheese and salami, I can do without.'

Tim saying, 'Suit yourself.' Going out into the hall, stepping into the lift that wasn't there.

Harry unable to believe they had moved so fast. Left him no time to change his mind.

The hotel manager calling up to his room, Harry just dozing off again, thinking, What is this, fucking Chinese water torture? The hotel manager saying, 'I think it would be best if you came down, sir. There's been an accident.'

Perfect English.

Like Jan Willem de Groot. Like every other fucker in Holland except that old dear, second day, in that cheese shop Tim was so keen about going in, the only time you'd know you were in a foreign country.

Jan Willem saying, 'Don't knock it, Harry, it's your future.'

Some club in Amsterdam, The Melkweg, loud psychedelic music, kids all out of their heads, Jan Willem's idea of a night out on the town, Harry saying, no, shouting in Jan Willem's ear, 'One more kid with a hygiene problem asks me I want to score, I swear I'm going to off the fucker.'

Don't knock it.

Better than perfect.

Tim saying, 'Could be, it's time to move on.'

Knowing Harry when he got like that.

Not wanting to blow the deal.

They had driven back to Den Haag in two cars, Harry going with Jan Willem, Jan Willem asking about Tim, how long they had been partners? Harry saying, 'What is this? You need my whole history before we make a deal? You need to know what books I have out on loan from the library.'

Jan Willem laughing, making light of it, 'It's a lot of money, Harry.'

'I'm not with you.'

'I like to deal one to one. Partnerships, people fall out, it creates complications.'

Coming along that section of the motorway out by the airport, where the runway goes over the road, you could see the 747s taxiing for take-off, wings sticking out over the road as they crossed the raised section, fucking huge, Harry knowing he would never understand how they got up in the air.

Harry saying, 'Don't beat about the bush, Jan Willem,'

knowing Jan Willem would understand exactly what he meant with his perfect fucking English.

Jan Willem saying, again, 'It's a lot of money, Harry.' Then, 'You ever have any problem in that direction, let me know, I can make a call.'

Jan Willem, long hair, could do with a wash, big bushy moustache, giving him the look.

Scruffy Dutch bastard.

Harry reaching across, taking a handful of Jan Willem's T-shirt up by the neck, twisting the fabric, tightening it till the shit had trouble breathing, Jan Willem saying, 'Fuck, Harry, I'm trying to drive!' Harry saying, 'We drop the subject.'

Releasing his grip, Jan Willem rubbing his neck, holding the Eldorado, a steady eighty, in the outside lane, one hand on the wheel.

'Okay, Harry,' he said. 'We drop the subject.'

Harry, now, lying in bed, his vest wet from the dream, not wanting to go any further into that weekend, glad when Celeste came into the room, switched on the main light, said, 'You awake, Harry?'

Watched her undress, take a shower, door open, he could see her through the glass, then towelling down, getting into bed, cupping his balls with her hand... and Harry was back in Den Haag, Tim cupping his balls, tongue in his mouth, Harry screaming, 'The fuck you doing?'

B ertram lay in the warm bath, holding himself, looking at the photographs of Gerry, of himself and Gerry, framed in gilt, remembering how they had always planned to re-do the bathroom, get rid of the Regency stripe, something pompeii, distressed, pale pinks, gold trim...

And blue.

Christ, was it almost two years, already!

His favourite, the two of them on a day out in Bognor Regis, trousers rolled up to the knee, icy cold water, sometime in February, that morning Gerry pulling the bedroom curtains on a clear blue winter sky, saying, 'Fuck work, let's go to the coast for the day.' Train from Victoria, change at Gatwick. Bognor

Regis so off the map it didn't have a direct service, let alone a motorway. Family-run Italian ice cream parlour just up past the pier along the front. Knickerbocker Glories. Stayed over at The Royal Norfolk Hotel, which king was it died there, last words, 'Bugger Bognor'? Whoever. Bertram and Gerry had arrived to haunt his words that night.

'No baggage?' the girl at reception had said.

Eight-thirty of a Monday night.

Boyfriend and a game of pool waiting for her down the Marlborough.

Who needed guests?

Bertram saying to Gerry, 'This place has seen better days.'

Gerry saying, while the receptionist waited for a response, 'Like the rest of Bognor. Therein lies its charm,' then to the girl, 'Baggage?'

The girl confused.

Gerry saying, 'Luggage, *not* Baggage. It may not seem so to you, but there is a world of difference between the two. Baggage implies excess, a burden, but, as you can see, we are not loaded down with the weight of any baggage,' grand flourish taking in the empty carpet around their feet, 'And, neither, do we have any luggage.'

Bertram, now, smiling.

Remembering how Gerry liked to go on.

The girl standing there, confusion replaced by boredom.

Gerry, sighing, saying to her, 'Where do we sign, dear.'

Trying the hot water tap, checking if the water in the immersion was hot enough for a top up. The taps, brass with pearl inlays, roman capitals, found them in a barn sale in Suffolk. The water, warm, then steaming, Bertram with his chin just above the surface, aroma of pine salts, trying, but failing, to relax... the first melanoma, before either of them had ever heard of AIDS.

Gerry: 'It's a mole.' Bertram saying, 'It wasn't there before, sweet.' In seven years, knowing every inch of Gerry's body, better than he knew his own. The pleurisy that nearly took him. Two years of disintegration, echoed by the revelations of the world's press, neither of them ever unfaithful, appalled by their legacy. The Ladbroke Grove Hospice, Solomon Wolfson Primary School, in just one decade transformed from a playground for young Jewish kids to a dormitory for the dying...

The final pneumonia, Gerry's body like parchment, consumed with cancer, Bertram at Gerry's bedside, was he hoping for some grand final speech, a whispered aphorism that could give comfort in the months of mourning to come? The short frantic breaths of his lover reminding him of every goldfish he had ever seen dying in a bowl.

Bertram never taking the test himself.

What was the point?

Stroking himself.

Thinking of Gerry, strong and healthy.

Not how he was at the end.

Seed spilling into the bath water.

Seed of death.

Seeing the woman's face, again.

The fear.

The scream, as he disappeared into the crowd, Ross with the daughter... the both of them thinking, What the fuck was Harry playing at?

Maybe it was time Harry stuffed his job.

Bertram sat up, pulled the plug, climbed out of the bath and wrapped himself in a towel. It was two-thirty a.m, and he needed to talk to somebody... anybody. Since Gerry died, since he'd cut himself off from everybody they knew, lived like a fucking monk, who was there? He trailed wet footprints through to the living room, poured himself a vodka, found his Filofax and dialled Sarah's number, waiting twenty rings, counted every one, before she answered, sounding stoned, or woken from a deep sleep. Another voice in the background, saying, 'Whoever it is, this time of night, tell them to fuck off.'

'Sarah?'

'Bertram?'

'Yes, it's me.'

'Bertram.'

'I'm in a bit of a state.'

'And you ring me? This time of night?'

'I never did it before.'

'That makes it okay?'

'Sarah.'

'Bertram, isn't Harry always telling you...'

'Yes, I know, I know, lay off the sulphates... I'm straight, Sarah, believe me.'

The other voice: 'Whoever it is, tell them to piss off.'

'Charming.'

'He has a point.'

Then, the sound of a scuffle, Sarah saying, 'Michael, give over, will you.' Worse, she giggled. Then the other voice, up close to the receiver, 'Listen, pal, swivel on this.'

Bertram saying, 'Only a fat-head would be waving his middle finger down a phone line.'

'*Fathead*? Are you serious?'

The line going dead.

The iguana, Noddy, staring at Bertram from his glass terrarium, taking up a whole corner of the living room, sat there on his log, waiting for the next fly to come buzzing. Present from Gerry, exotic pet shop in Parkway, had him five years, fuck knows how old he was, if he was a he even, only command he ever learnt was, 'Stay'.

The iguana blinked.

Slow motion.

'What the fuck do you know, Noddy,' Bertram said.

Staring at the phone.

The whole world a variety of combinations away.

Who does he ring?

The girl who types his letters.

Goes for sandwiches.

Saying to himself:

'Bertram, you're a pathetic bastard.'

Ross in a window seat, but couldn't see through it for the steam. Cafe on the corner of Westbourne Grove and Monmouth Road, family business, Germans, hot *bratwurst* and *eintopf*, nice continental pastries, till four-thirty in the morning, only place for miles open this time of night… brewed a decent coffee, too. Ross on his second cup, going easy on the sugar after what Mary said about his gut this morning, wondering if he should go to the counter, order some soup, slice of rye bread; whatever it was Mary had left in the oven earlier, he wasn't going to feel like eating when he got in. Traffic would be light, he could be back in Finsbury Park fifteen minutes, no sweat, but Ross unwilling to get moving, thinking about the girl in the park and, now, this other girl, couldn't be older than seventeen, two tables down, nursing an empty tea mug since Ross arrived in the place, holdall down by her chair, rolling one cigarette just as soon as she'd finished the last one – Ross hadn't seen them rolled that thin since he had been on the inside.

The girl, now, grabbing her holdall, Ross noticing one of the handles was broken, coming over to Ross's table, sitting down, saying, 'They're going to chuck me out if I don't order something.'

Ross saying, 'So?'

The girl saying, 'The price of a cup of tea not going to break you, is it?'

A queue building up at the counter – waiters, musicians, hotel staff, finished work, getting something to eat on the way home. Two young blokes, still in their office suits, been on the piss since five-thirty, couldn't decide which pastry to have with their coffee, holding up the queue, but no harm to anyone…

Ross saying, 'You didn't smoke so much, you could afford to buy your own tea.' Thinking about the other girl, the little girl in the park, her father finally getting his order in at the bar, taking his eyes off her while he paid for the drink, the girl saying, 'What about my drink,' the father not hearing, still counting out change. Ross taking her hand, telling her, 'Your mum will get you a drink, she says I'm to take you back to her.'

Walking her across the main concourse, the stalls all closing down, the clown on stilts handing out the last of the balloons, Ross taking one for the girl. Lifting her over the low fence, carrying her across where the putting green was in the summer…

The little girl saying, 'This isn't the way.'

Starting to cry.

The girl with him, now, saying, 'Full of the milk of human kindness, you are.'

'I didn't ask you to sit here.'

Pretty eyes, but a thin mouth. Brown hair, too curly to be attractive as long as it was. Wearing a beige, double-breasted driver's jacket, catalogue job, she must have picked it up in a charity shop.

The girl rolling another cigarette, Ross saying, 'How come you've no money?'

'Train fare was more than I thought.'

'Where from?'

'Darlington.'

Pulling a face.

'Darlington? So what happened to the accent?'

'I don't *come* from Darlington, give me a break. The folks moved up there two years ago, only the old man was happy about it, got himself a job in an electronics factory, they made parts for the Royal Navy, so he said, radar and stuff. We're from New Cross, originally, that's where I was brought up.'

'Must have been hard on you.'

'And the rest! Darlington's a dump.'

Ross finished his coffee, said, 'You have any family in London, friends you can stay with?'

'If only.'

She undid her coat, only a T-shirt underneath, black, with the name of a band in fluorescent pink, The Buzzcocks. Ross surprised at the fullness of her bosom, thinking, Mary was the first, and only Mary since, how would it be with another woman. Not this girl, barely seventeen...

The little girl in the park, holding her in the shadows beneath the trees, the balloon drifting up into the night sky, acrid with smoke from the fireworks and the bonfire, seeing her parents appear on the main concourse, the woman shouting at the man, the man hurrying off down the concourse, Ross saying, 'See, there's your mother, over there, go on, run.'

Releasing the girl.

The girl, now, saying, 'I'm still a virgin and want to keep it that way, but I do a good suck.'

Mary never did that. Ungodly, she said.

Remembering Harry, bar in South London, somewhere, this woman all over him, saying to her, 'Only thing interests me, darling, do you spit or do you swallow?'

Ross telling himself he hadn't hurt the girl, hadn't really even frightened her very much, it was no big deal, but still, how was he not supposed to feel bad about it?

Saying to this girl, 'Do you still want another cup of tea?'

'I've had two regular boyfriends. They both said I do it better than anybody.'

Ross standing up, looking down at the girl. Seventeen? Fuck, fifteen, more like. Saying, 'What's your name?'

'Chrissie.'

'Well, Chrissie, I'm parked just down the road.'

Outside, on the pavement, he turned to the girl, pulled a crisp twenty from his wallet, put it in her hand.

'I can't help you, Chrissie.'

'What's this for?'

'Conscience money. Call it twenty Hail Mary's. Get yourself a room.'

Watched her go back into the German cafe.

Sit down with the two pissheads…

Never made it home from the office.

Earlier, before the day turned from bad to worse, Mandy going walkabout at the firework display, Denise getting paranoid, screaming, 'This is your doing, Giles, you and that bitch!', Giles had been thinking, Do I need this? Do I really, really need this?

In Graeme's office, not even offered a seat, Graeme saying, 'I know you want the job, Giles. The blunt truth is, you're not ready. Chris, for all his faults, had drive, he was an innovator.'

'And public school.'

'What does that mean?'

From where he was standing, Giles could see down into Covent Garden, the Piazza, wondered what it must have looked like when it was still a market, vegetable stalls, flat-top lorries loading up, porters with their barrows stacked with boxes, wholesalers calling out current prices, marking them on a chalkboard… another world, was it really only ten years ago?

'Breeding,' Giles said. 'How do you see me, Graeme? Grammar School upstart, useful up to a point, just as long as he doesn't get ideas above his station?'

Amazed that he was saying this.

Graeme, equally amazed, saying, 'You do a good job, Giles, I wouldn't want to lose you.'

'But, wouldn't lose too much sleep if you did.'

'If I may say so, this approach is likely to prove entirely unproductive.'

Chris on the phone, earlier, Giles just got in, not even time to sit down at his desk, 'A word in your ear, old time's sake and all that. Heard it down the grapevine, Simon Mates has been offered the job.'

Simon Mates?

The question unstated, Chris continuing, 'Features writer on *Venue*, buddy of Graeme's from way back when.'

Giles so sure he would be offered the job.

Graeme saying, 'Would be incredibly grateful, if you could handle some of Chris's work load, manuscripts, tying in the visuals, that kind of thing, just till we get settled.' Now, saying, 'Giles, for God's sake, sit down. There seems to have been some terrible breakdown in communication between us.'

Giles, still standing, saying, 'It's quite simple, Graeme. In order to get me to help cover for Chris, you led me to believe I might be in with a chance.'

'I made no such promise.'

'Not in so many words, no.'

Rachel, Graeme's PA poking her head round the door, saying, 'Graeme, you're five minutes late for the editorial meeting… they're all in there waiting.'

Colin Bird, the Art Editor.

John Devereaux, Circulation Manager.

Mark Smith, Sales Director.

Graeme standing in for Chris, for his replacement, hadn't been to an editorial meeting for eighteen months, before he booted Chris.

Telling Rachel, 'Well, let them wait,' looking at Giles, 'this is important.'

After the door had closed, Giles saying, 'Didn't you always say, "Second-class magazine written by third-rate journalists"?'

'You're losing me.'

'*Venue*.'

Graeme laughing, 'God, yes. What a hoo-ha that all was. Good for us, mind you, all over the Dailies for two weeks, editorial spreads in the weekend supplements, "Listings War Hots Up," then the bloody Falklands came along, still, good while it lasted, though.'

'You were worried at the time.'

'You really think so? Gaggle of co-operative malcontents, you really expect them to survive in the real world? First week, circulation of thirty-five thousand, six months later, down to ten. I'm surprised they've lasted this long, it's only because the bloody Labour Party is underwriting their loses.'

'So, you hold them in such disregard, why are you offering Simon Mates the job?'

Aware that Graeme was genuinely dumbfounded.

'Simon Mates?'

'That's what I heard.'

'Simon Mates is a real ale-fuelled tit-wit who should never have got beyond reviewing folk albums by uillean pipe players born somewhere north of Cumbria – where on earth did you pick up this actionable gossip?'

Giles thinking, Chris, you bastard.

Would you really do this to me?

Knowing the answer.

'It's not true?'

Graeme making the most of the moment, saying, 'You know, Giles, there are times when I wished I stilled smoked.'

Giles, nothing more to say.

'That magical hiatus, how on earth do you fill it. Picture me lighting up, leaning back in my chair, taking a deep drag.' Then, 'Giles, you've made an arsehole of yourself, am I right?'

Rearguard action.

'You can understand, Simon Mates. How could I take that lying down?'

'More important, you could actually believe I would employ an idiot like that.'

'I should have given it more thought.'

'Yes, indeed.'

Denise in with Mandy, vowed she wouldn't let her out of her sight, even when they got down to Barbara's. Giles, alone in the bed, hearing Graeme fucking Tate's final words, 'Believe me, Giles, I'll know when you're ready.'

Fuck it!

Denise on the phone for hours when they got back, how long did it take to arrange a trip? Giles telling her it was term time, Denise shouting, 'When was it you ever concerned yourself with term time. What class is Mandy in, go on, Giles, just tell me that.'

The smell of firework smoke still in Giles's nose, pouring a glass of red wine, saying, 'But, it was going so well, between us, better than it's ever been,' thinking of last night, Denise doing something down there, tightening her muscles, like a tight warm glove, Giles not able to hold back, coming before Denise was ready, but feeling okay about it because he knew that was how Denise meant it to be. Then, going down on her, Christ, when was the last time he did that, every time he did it with somebody else thinking, Why don't I do this with Denise?

Still feeling...

What?

Embarrassed...

When she came.

Clawing his back.

Pulling his hair.

Thinking, 'Denise, don't. You'll wake Mandy.'

Wondering what it would feel like to be told you had a fatal disease. Couldn't be worse than this.

*B*itterballen.
Or, *bittenballen*?
Harry couldn't remember which they were called.
Like scotch eggs to look at, little ones, you ate them from a bowl with your beer. Brown crusty skin, inside, meat gravy and melted cheese, hot enough to burn the roof of your mouth out.

The second night...

Jan Willem saying they would like this bar, The Post Horn, Den Haag, just east of the Centrum, the main shopping precinct, Harry and Tim, Jan Willem de Groot with his girl-friend, Petra. Tim saying to Harry, just after they were intro-duced, 'Hope she hasn't got any sisters.'

Jan Willem playing tour guide, the Eldorado parked in a paved square, trees around the perimeter, pointing through the trees to the bar, big double frontage, parade of expensive shops facing into the square, saying, 'A very traditional Dutch bar, very old. German officers liked to drink here during the Occupation,' spitting a great gob on to the pavement as he said, 'German officers.' Petra saying, 'Jan Willem!' Jan Willem laugh-ing, 'We are among friends, no?' Beyond the square, across the Mainstraat and the tram lines, the Royal Palace and floodlit fountains.

'Very up-market area, lots of *nouvelle cuisine* restaurants – not a place to come if you are hungry!'

Laughing, again.

The bar, high ceiling, columns, dark wood panel and carpet, everything nicotine-brown, waiter service only, the waiters in white shirts and bow ties, the clientele mostly old couples, family groups, all comfortably off, Harry noticing the women always sat with their arms folded, like they were running out of patience, ready to leave… Jan Willem ordering the *bitterballen*.

Or, *bittenballen*.

Saying, 'You won't find these in McDonalds,' then, looking around, 'You prefer this to the Melkweg?'

Tim saying, 'Somewhere between the two there has to be a happy medium.'

Jan Willem laughing.

Again.

Harry wondering if he was going to laugh every time he spoke, stained teeth, from the Gauloise he always had stuck in his fat mouth, Jan Willem saying, 'The night is young, Tim. Relax, you will have your fun.'

The Heineken beer, on draft, much stronger than in England, then the Jenever. Jan Willem explaining that there was 'old' Jenever and 'young' Jenever, Dutch gin, you drank it neat in shot glasses, Harry couldn't tell any difference between the two, either one of them could blow your fucking head off, more than a few glasses.

Petra, nursing a fruit juice, not saying much, putting her hand over her glass every time a fresh round was ordered, now making signs that she wanted to go. Jan Willem checking his watch, calling for the bill, while the waiter was at the cashier's desk, and Petra in the cloakroom, saying, 'My girl, she has to be up early. Some of us have to work for a living.'

Tim saying, 'Bundle of laughs, your Petra.'

Jan Willem laughing, again, his eyes on Tim, not sure how to take him. Then Jan Willem driving them over to the south side of the city, dropping Petra off, Petra saying, 'Pleased to have met you.'

Driving away from her apartment building, Jan Willem saying, 'Now I will show you my home town, the real Den Haag.' Harry too pissed now to know where the fuck they were.

Remembering a cellar bar full of kids, cubby-holes with couples all over each other, stank of dope. Jan Willem pointing out a geezer sat on a high stool at the end of the bar, looked Algerian, selling shit, open as you like, little cellophane packets like they gave you in the bank for small change, a single dope leaf, like a palm tree, printed in green on one side, custom manufactured. Five guilders or ten guilders – Tim called them 'gliders' – the amount you got depended on the quality of the dope.

Jan Willem saying, 'It's no big thing, Harry. I take you to a place tomorrow, coffee bar, down by the canal, they give you a menu. Red, black, Afghan, Moroccan, whatever you want, you just order it like you were ordering an espresso.'

The Algerian recognising Jan Willem, saying, 'Hey! Jan the Man,' Harry thinking, Didn't these fuckers ever speak their own language, even to each other?

Tim giving the chat to two Australian birds, on the world tour, working the bars across Europe, hoped to be in London – London Town, they called it – by the autumn. Tim getting to that stage, 'So what's it like, doing it in a Volkswagen Camper?' Then, 'Can't do a lot for the suspension, you two anything to go by.' Like bees to the honey, the birds always like that with Tim.

One of them, Loren, saying, 'Hey, if all the Pommy blokes are like you, I can't wait to get there.'

Jan Willem cutting in, saying, 'Tim, don't waste your time, tonight is my treat, I have something special lined up.'

Laughing.

Harry drunk enough now for it to hurt every time Jan Willem laughed, thinking, Fuck me, you get stoned in here just breathing.

Jan Willem saying, 'Okay, boys, time to go window shopping.'

Out into the night air.

Dark streets, cobbled road.

Harry and Tim both having trouble staying on the narrow pavement.

Turning into a brighter street, the light coming from shop windows, curtains pulled open, girls sitting in easy chairs in the windows, comfortable rooms, big double beds, Harry had heard about it, but never seen it before, surprised how good-looking the girls were, a long way from the burnt out cases, slags every one of them, you saw up Kings Cross.

Jan Willem, saying, 'Take your pick, a present from me to you, to cement our relationship.'

Tim giggling, 'How about a T in a B, then, Harry, fancy that?' Taking a piss in the gutter, couldn't give a fuck. Jan Willem puzzled, Harry saying, 'Your English not so fucking perfect after all, eh, Jan Willem?'

This time, Harry and Tim laughing.

Harry going along with Tim's idea, thinking he could take a back seat, watch TV, have another drink, while Tim got on with it, not get involved at all, if he was lucky. Screwing whores wasn't Harry's idea of a night out. You had to pay for it, there had to be something wrong. Besides, he had Celeste back home...

Who in his right fucking mind needed to look at another woman after Celeste?

The whore said her name was Rina, half-Indonesian, drop-dead beautiful, in a turquoise dress, long sheath skirt, slits up to the thigh, laughing with Harry and Tim, explaining to Jan Willem, T in a B, they were talking Three in a Bed, so he could negotiate with the house management before fucking off and leaving them to it.

Rina insisting they both took a shower, there were dressing gowns they could wear. Pulling the drape curtains on the street, the room looking like any five star hotel room, Rina sensing Harry wasn't really interested, working on Tim, while Harry sat across the room, TV on loud, trying not to notice how ridiculous Tim's arse looked, pumping up and down like that on the bed, Rina going, 'Baby, baby,' Harry could have been fooled into thinking she was enjoying it.

Then the two of them giggling, whispering, coming over to where Harry was sitting, Rina undoing his dressing gown.

Tim making his move...

Later, in his room at The Wilhelmina, Harry ringing Jan Willem, waking him from a deep sleep, saying, 'You know what you were on about yesterday, me and Tim?' Jan Willem, not laughing now, taking a while to understand.

Fucker must have known he was pissed.

Harry remembering sending Ross out there, after the deal was set in concrete, everything working like clockwork, Tim in the ground six months, telling Ross, 'Break laughing boy's fucking neck for me, will you.'

Celeste always asking, 'One day you're going to have to tell me, Harry what really happened with Tim.'

How could he?

Horrified.

His prick going stiff

Tim's fucking tongue in his mouth.

Chapter 6
That wriggled and wriggled,
And wriggled inside her...

Giles and Denise arguing, Denise with Mandy, holding her close in the back, Giles trying not to catch her eye every time he checked the rear-view mirror, thinking, There had to be a better world...

New Range Rover, well, not this year's registration – one previous owner, only forty-two thousand on the clock, the salesman, David Lord's of Henley, saying, 'This motor? You could take it round the clock twice, it would still tow a 747 down the runway for you.'

Fuck the repayments, fuck Graeme Tate and, without having to lick his arse, didn't bear thinking about – this should be an enjoyable experience.

Despite, he still would have preferred the Porsche.

Giving in to Denise.

How could he not, this business with Celeste blowing up in his face?

Who was it, anyway...

Making all the money?

Denise's argument, not this one, another one two weeks back: 'Your crowd? What's wrong with your crowd? Where do I start about your crowd!'

Giles trying to watch *Sports Night* on the TV, QPR about to lose again in the last five minutes of the match, Giles willing the referee to blow his whistle, despite he already knew the final score from the news earlier.

Denise saying, 'Let me tell you about your crowd... the important thing with your crowd is, they always have to be the first on to something then, the first to drop it – great sense of timing, but not much else.'

Denise's idea of a Porsche.

Green framed glasses.

Late night chat show hosts.

Slum landlords, living off benefits.

A&R men.

Photographers…

Déclassé.

Giles saying, 'Okay, you've made your point.' Then: 'So, who's the snob around here, anyway?'

'Don't you wish you could be… naturally?' Denise had said.

Coming off the Marylebone overpass, missed the turn-off for Paddington Station, Denise too busy bending his ear, stuck in the tail-back down off the elevated section into Marylebone Road, Giles thinking, Bottle-green, not a scratch, black leather and walnut trim, best of all, the way you sat up there looking down on everybody else on the road…

V-eight, auto transmission, drive-select.

Happy days?

So help me.

Saying to Denise, 'How many more times do we have to go through this?'

Council official, yellow fluorescent armband, Amenities Department, considered himself a trouper, working after dark … then the policeman, younger than Giles and Denise, fresh faced, uncomfortable in his uniform, Christ! Giles thinking, Imagine when the judges look that young – the policeman, no weight of authority, saying, 'After all, no harm done.'

Denise: 'No harm done? My child abducted by a perfect stranger and you stand there and say, "No harm done?"'

'If there was a stranger, mam.'

'And the man in the watch cap, the one who spoke to me?'

Giles saying, 'Denise, you need to hear yourself, you're being paranoid.'

'Just as likely your little girl wandered off, thought she might get into trouble…'

'Made it up, you mean?'

Giles saying, '*Are* you lying, Mandy?'

Denise: 'Of course she's not!'

Mandy crying.

The policeman: 'Put it down to a fertile imagination.'

The amenities officer: 'We're going to have to leave by the south gate.'

The policeman saying he would report the incident.

Denise, 'And?'

'I doubt anything will come of it.'

Denise, now, in the car saying, 'You don't see the connection, Giles. Are you blind, or just stupid?'

Giles, knowing his first right filter was Baker Street, maybe a left at Madame Tussaud's, cross the Edgware Road, back where he would have been if he hadn't missed the turn-off. Lost twenty minutes, fuck London, fuck the traffic, fuck Denise, saying, 'Don't be so bloody ridiculous – you think Celeste's husband is a madman?'

Denise: 'How do you know he isn't?'

Giles: 'How are we for time?'

Denise: 'You don't see it, do you, Giles?'

Giles shifting out of automatic into second gear, just for something to do, saying, 'While you're down there, you see Jack, that's it, you understand that?'

Mandy listening to all this, her mother's arm tight around her shoulder, Denise saying, despite it was the last thing she wanted right now, 'Don't tempt me, Giles.'

Ross arrived at the Bright's place, row of terraced houses, off Lillie Road, at the same time as the hearse. There was one other limousine, that, and the hearse, both Austin Princesses. Stink of fireworks, from last night, still in the air, pall-bearers in ill-fitting suits, standing around outside on the pavement, hands behind their backs, looked like they were all dying for a smoke. The hearse piled high with wreaths, you could hardly see the coffin, biggest one in the back window, pride of place, mixture of white daisies and pink chrysanthemum, set in a laurel surround, reading: 'We'll Meet Again'.

Knowing the flowers from too many other times.

Acknowledging the taste in music.

What the fuck if Vera Lynn was a Brit?

Good music was good music.

Full stop.

Ross drove past where the limousines were parked, found somebody pulling out, fifty yards up, on the right hand side, backing into the space, one move, thinking, Do I really fucking need this… a funeral? Cut the ignition, the rear view and offside wing mirrors not giving him enough scope, turning in his seat, saw the kid coming out of the house, would hardly have recognised him. Ray Benjamin Bright, nineteen, unemployed, and the rest – according to Bertram – wearing a dark sports jacket, white shirt, dark brown tie, dressed like he was going for a job interview. Helping an old girl with a tight perm and a walking stick out of a Metro, the two of them met on the doorstep by an older man, Sunday Best suit, had to be Ray's old man, the old girl being helped up the step into the house.

Neighbours all at their bay windows or out at the front gate. Ross glad that he wasn't driving the Roller. Harry had finally seen sense, bunged him the cash to pick up something a bit less obvious, needing another motor, anyway, the Roller out of service for a week having new windows fitted. Audi 2000s, four door saloon, bodywork seen better days, but, what the fuck, who hadn't? Ross had taken it over to Desmond's lock-up, New Cross... wouldn't be seen dead when Millwall were at home. Specialised in insurance write-offs, acetylene torch jobs, straight down the middle – new coat of paint, any fucker didn't know better, he was welcome. Desmond had given it the once-over, taps, valves, what the fuck did Ross know about modern motors, assured Ross it would do the business, despite looking like a heap of shit.

Everybody coming out of the house, now, Ross surprised at how many of them there were. The immediate family, six of them, including Ray, getting into the Austin Princess, the others, finding their own cars, taking forever getting all the doors unlocked, everybody pulling handles that wouldn't open. Then the cars all out in the road, the hearse moving off, the funeral director walking in front to the end of the road, then climbing into the front passenger seat of the hearse.

Ross followed the cortege... Putney Bridge, Barnes Common, Sheen Road, to Mortlake.

The Crematorium.

Parked away from the others, big circular gravel driveway, another group of mourners waiting to go in, Ross thinking, Everybody happy to fucking queue to the death. Locked the car, walked across the grass, stood looking out at the river beyond the tow path, feeling the cold. There were two craft out on the water, a rowing eight, school kids, drifting with the current, oars shipped, cox in an outboard dingy, megaphone

'I'll give you the full story – phone rings, I hear it because I'm not asleep, despite I'm tired as fuck. I go pick it up, this kid's voice says, "Celeste there?" I say, "Celeste? Do I know you?" The kid says, "No, but we do both have something in common…"'

'Harry…'

'I say, "Oh, really, what's that?" You know what he says?'

Celeste just listening.

'"We both fuck your wife," that's what he said to me.'

'Jesus Christ, Harry, what did you say to him?'

Harry smiled.

'I told him he should sober up, call you back in the morning.'

raised, giving them what for, Ross not able to make out the words... the kids in vests and shorts, they must be fucking freezing out there, still preferring it to being stuck in a class-room.

Ross hating them for just being kids.

Remembering Pat Ryan's boat, Dingle Bay, twelve footer, used to row out six miles, the weather was right, Ross just a kid, himself, then, horrified when he hauled in a drowned Cormorant that must have dived into the water, got itself trapped in Pat's fishing net.

Saw Ray's family going in.

Walked across to the building.

Smoke rising.

Stood in the doorway of the chapel.

The vicar, from the pulpit, reading a burial sermon – hesitat-ing on the 'she', not wanting to fuck up – 'gone to a better place,' the name, 'Louisa', dropped in, a pause to glance at his notes... the coffin sat there, curtains behind, waiting to be rolled into the furnace, it could have been anybody...

Cahersiven...

The wake.

His mother laid out on the dining table in the parlour, Ross touching her cheek when nobody else was in the room, repelled by the coldness, reminded of wax... his mother. The kitchen a social club, the whole town, it seemed, everybody Ross had ever known, passing through, going into the other room, staying a while, there in the dark with the candles. The priest known her thirty years, christened all her children, buried her husband, when they brought him back from the prison mortuary. Ross's sisters crying, his brothers saying to each other, and to Ross, 'You all right, then?' When it was time, the brothers carrying the coffin to the church, then the grave-yard... fresh dug earth, that smell, piled to one side, each of them, in turn, taking a handful of earth, throwing it down on the coffin, Ross hurting most because he wouldn't cry...

Why the fuck not?

Remembering the graveyard, the steep slope leading down into the valley, the grey rectangular slabs of the communal graves, from The Famine, one end open, you could see the bones in there, used to be a dare, you would crawl in there, when Ross was a kid... alongside them, grand marble tombstones, ten feet tall some of them, rich relatives over from the States, searching out their ancestry, commissioning these grand memorials to their long dead relatives, let everybody know the family had made good over the water.

Remembering his youngest sister, Siobhán, saying, 'You look like you're doing well for yourself, Ross.'

Three children of her own by then.

Now? Ross had lost count.

Lost touch.

Ross saying, 'I wish I could get over more often.'

Siobhán saying, 'Sure, Ross, I'll be seeing you at my own funeral, and that's the truth.'

Piped organ music, *Abide With Me*, the curtains opening, the coffin rolling back, disappearing, Ross thinking, Louisa Bright, that was your life. Stood back as the family came out of the chapel, the vicar shaking hands, the family walking slowly around the ornamental pool to where the floral tributes were on display in a paved garden area, raised beds, plaque on the wall, read, 'Garden of Remembrance'. Some of them bending down, reading the cards, checking who had sent what, spent how much. Ray's old man talking to another man, slightly older, could have been a brother, discussing whether they should sort out the flowers themselves, 'I know it's awkward, time like this…'

'They said to me they gave them to the Charing Cross Hospital… brighten up the wards.'

'Well, just so long as they do.'

The old girl with the perm and the walking stick, joining them, saying to Ray's old man, 'Lou's wedding ring, George, you didn't forget to ask them for the wedding ring.'

Ross thinking, Stroll on!

Moving through the group.

Standing beside Ray.

A woman saying, 'I do hate it when they leave them in the cellophane.'

Another: 'What did she do to deserve it… the way she had to suffer.'

Ross saying to Ray, 'A word in your ear.'

The kid turning to face him.

Full frontal.

Ross liked that.

Then the kid spoiling it by holding out his hand, assuming Ross was some relative he didn't recognise.

Ross ignoring the hand, saying, 'That hammer, fifteen-pounder? What I would call a regular piece of housebreaking equipment.'

The kid's expression not changing, saying, 'Who the fuck are you.'

Wondering if he was a copper.

Knowing they came to funerals.

Dead cert you would find somebody you were looking for at a family funeral. The mugs couldn't keep away, thought they had some special dispensation, one of their own to bury.

Ross saying, 'Take your time, you'll get there.'

Not crowding the kid, but still he stepped back a pace, looking around Ross to where the family were standing around, the funeral director making motions for them to leave, Ray's old man saying to him, 'If you want to come back for a drink, you're more than welcome,' the funeral director saying, 'Very kind of you, perhaps just a quick one,' Ray saying to Ross, 'Think we got to go.'

Ross saying, remembering that cold touch, 'You only ever have one mother, Ray.'

Ray saying, 'Thank fuckin' christ for that.'

Harry on the phone to Tingo Maria.

Whoever it was at the other end having a lot of trouble locating Nestor. Harry thinking, Fucking fortune this call is costing me. Hearing the echo of shoes on stone floors, big rooms, picturing how hot it must be out there right now, despite they had probably just finished breakfast, three o'clock, raining again, in London.

Then Nestor saying, 'Harry, good to hear.'

Good to hear?

Maybe the Dutch weren't so bad to deal with, after all.

Harry saying, 'About coming over next week, I've been thinking.'

Nestor saying, 'We got it all arranged, everybody is very excited. My wife, she's been looking forward to it since I told her about you, just a little bit worried you going to like her cooking.'

Harry thinking, Am I hearing this? Is this the same fucking membrane-deficient psychopath I spent time with in New York? Snuff movies... big joke, some prat-fall waiting for the right Broadway production, phone call from Hollywood, in the meantime, shoots his own prick off.

Maybe he had the wrong number.

Every other fucker in Tingo Maria probably called Nestor.

Before he made the call, knowing exactly how he was going to put it...

No sweat.

Except, for the first time in his life, Harry was not feeling so sure about a lot of things.

Not about *what* he was doing.

About the *way* he was doing them.

Try explaining that to a greaser wanted to introduce you to his wife's home cooking.

'Is this a cold foot, Harry?'

Jesus Christ, Mother of Mary!

'Nestor, if by "cold foot" you mean am I having second thoughts, then the answer is "no".'

'Second thoughts; it's not easy, Harry, you don't talk my kind of English.'

Oh shit.

Wanting to say:

Your kind of English?

Instead, saying, 'You know how it goes, Nestor. Things come up, you have to deal with them.'

'I get you, Harry.'

'It's just, I have to be here right now... now is not the right time.'

Nestor saying, 'Harry, this is not a small matter. What I'm saying, there are other people involved.'

'I'm hearing you, Nestor.'

'I hope so. Sometimes, it's not easy making yourself understood.'

Harry saying, 'Give my apologies to your wife, yeah? I'm sure she's gone to a lot of trouble.'

Nestor saying, 'Fuck the wife, Harry.'

Giles had just known that Jane, if he ever did get round to putting it to her, would be one of those vocal bitches, panting loudly in his ear just as soon as he touched her, embarrassing him, saying things like, 'Do it now! Do it now!' and 'Oh God! That feels so good,' thrashing beneath him and clawing at his back – a long, long way from Giles's idea of a quiet, clandestine afternoon fuck.

Lying with her in his and Denise's bed, Jane taking him in her hand saying, 'Isn't he an itsy-witsy spoilsport?' She would have to be leaving in half an hour, Onya, the au pair, would have picked up Kate from after-care, would need help with her and little Terry while she got the dinner started, Peter always back prompt at six-fifteen, expected his dinner on the table, bottle of red wine breathing, preferably something that reminded him of one of their Italian holidays… Jane coaxing Giles, wanting him to do it one more time before she had to shower, get dressed. Giles hating it when grown women adopted that little girl simper… a complete turn off.

Jane saying, 'Janey is going to have to think of a nickname for Giles's itsy-witsy, isn't she?' Then, 'What does Denise call him. Already, I hate her, the bitch.'

Giles saying, 'What hope for the sisterhood, eh? Have you no shame?'

'Lots and lots and lots,' Jane breathing, not saying, close to his ear.

Giles, now, wishing he had never rung her from the Magazine, just after lunch, blaming that third pint, Jane saying, 'You rang,' surprised, but not that surprised, Giles saying, 'I put Denise and Mandy on the train to Aberystwyth this a.m. What are you doing this afternoon?'

Jane saying, 'You don't waste any time.'

Giles: 'Strike while the iron is hot?'

Jane: 'Mmm! Fantasies, fantasies, my very own sweaty blacksmith.'

'Complete with leather apron.'

Giles asking Rachel to tell Graeme he would be out of the office all afternoon, had fixed up to see the Civic Auditor, that business with the Council and the Petticoat Lane graft, knowing Graeme would be only too happy for him to be shit-shovelling when it involved a Liberal-controlled council.

Jane, now, saying, 'Itsy-witsy doesn't want to play. Is there a magic word… does Denise know the magic word?'

Still coaxing him.

Giles thinking, Why the fuck doesn't she just go down and get on with it? Saying, 'Denise isn't like that. She doesn't have a pet name.'

Neither did Celeste.

And with Celeste, it – whatever Jane decided to fucking call it – wouldn't have needed any coaxing.

Surprised, his prick coming to life.

Just thinking about Celeste.

Fucking bitch.

Jane, 'Oh! Itsy-witsy has turned into Mr Biggy-Wiggy!'

Giles thinking, Jesus Christ!

Blaming Denise.

This was all her fault.

If she hadn't been in the bath last night when Jane rang… something about Kate's Natural Resource project, Kate in tears because she couldn't find it, frightened that she would get into trouble with her teacher at school tomorrow, she hadn't, by any chance, left it round there that afternoon when they dropped Mandy off?

'You know how children get over silly things?'

Jane straddling him, knees tight against Giles's ribcage, with her hand, guiding him into her, arching her back, head thrown back as she began to move, saying, 'Oh me, oh my!'

Giles watching her heavy breasts.

Bringing his hands up to cover them.

Jane, last night on the phone, saying, 'Something of an honour, Giles, getting to speak to you… we don't see very much of you these days.'

Giles, knowing Jane had always been on the cards.

It was just a matter of when. If ever.

Saying, 'I do hope it hasn't left too much of a hole in your life.'

Jane, in tune, immediately.

Saying, 'Valium helps.' Then, 'You can't blame a girl for dreaming.'

Laughing.

To pass it off as a joke, if necessary.

Peter, in the background, saying, 'Who's that you're talking to, darling?'

Jane saying, 'Denise.'

That moment.

The Rubicon.

Giles saying, 'Jane, I should call you, sometime.'

Jane saying, 'Don't leave it too long.'

Now, coming, in a series of 'Whoops!'

Each one louder than than the last.

Giles thinking he would have trouble with the neighbours, she didn't stop soon.

Then thinking, Why, oh why, oh why?

B ertram had often wondered, over the years – if he was going to kill himself, *had* to kill himself, for whatever reason, how would he go about it?

A game.

A macabre fantasy.

Never serious… Bertram always believing that suicide was, at best, the ultimate cop-out, the easy option. Viewed in a less kind light, guilty, every time, he could be so bloody minded, thinking, The ultimate indulgence…

Ego sum.

Till Gerry died.

His usual table, he didn't need to reserve it any more, same date, every year, before and after Gerry died, this time, a Tuesday. Lorenzo, attentive as ever, he only had to smile in Bertram's direction for Bertram to remember Gerry saying, '"Lorenzo?" You have to be joking. Let's put a bet on it…'

His name. Anything but Lorenzo.

Gerry saying, 'Don't look so worried… do you think I would spoil our night?'

Bertram, never sure.

Trattoria Lorenzo. New Kings Road.

A walk from Bertram's maisonette, Dionus Road, how they both laughed about that, when Gerry moved in.

Gerry, saying, 'Sounds like an anagram for Adonis,' holding Bertram, whispering, 'Beautiful young boy.' And, 'Not that far from Dionysus, either, Greek god of wine.'

Classical education.

His parents, for all their Bloomsbury Set affectations, devastated when he was sent down in his second year at King's College, 'gross misconduct,' they never wanted to think what that meant. Gerry going into rep, his parents finally making their peace after seeing him up there on the big screen. The Gaumont, Hampstead, two lines in an Ealing Comedy starring Ian Carmichael, Gerry specialising in playing twits, in a sports jacket and cravat, climbing in and out of Austin Healey sports cars. In one of those rare moments when Gerry was down, saying to Bertram, 'I could have gone on from there... I could have been another Denholm Elliot.'

Another time, one Sunday afternoon, the two of them hysterical, watching a Battle of Britain film on the TV, black and white, John Gregson the star... Gerry's Spitfire going down in flames, you just knew it was going to happen after the big deal he made saying goodbye to his pet Labrador, Nellie, on the runway, before take off. Gerry saying, over the intercom, 'Looks like I've bought it, chaps.' His Spitfire exploding into a fireball.

Bertram saying, 'Christ, you looked such a dork in those days. I would never have fancied you.' Both of them in tears, from laughing.

Gerry saying, 'From Beaujolais to Mouton Cadet... it's our mutual good fortune you go for the older man.'

Bertram, now, smiling.

His meal finished

The same meal every year.

Melon to start.

No ginger – Lorenzo would kick you out of his restaurant, you asked for ginger on the melon. Then Gerry's favourite, Bertram himself not caring much for shellfish, ordering it for Gerry, part of the ritual: *Insalata di Mare*, remembering Gerry, holding a mussel, pointing to a barnacle he'd spotted on the shell, saying, 'I don't know why I'm eating this. Witness this tiny crustacean, most certainly dead, without the shadow of a doubt a rotting organism, can you imagine, all those bacteria, breeding in the sauce?'

Then: 'A positive rush of microscopic creepy-crawlies.'

Adding: 'One day, there will be a mussel with my name on it.'

Not so.

Lorenzo saying, 'Everything satisfactory, sir?'

Bertram saying, 'Marvellous.'

Recalling how Gerry used to love it when he was recognised from an advert on TV, small part in a cop show, never from his earlier film roles, Bertram himself would not have recognised him from them.

Lorenzo saying, 'Anything to follow... the sweet trolley, perhaps?'

Bertram: 'Just an espresso...

'And a grappa.'

Then the second grappa.

Never more than two.

Running through the options.

Discreet... or, flamboyant.

Suicide.

Discreet was a bottle of scotch and whatever pills could be stockpiled without the doctor becoming suspicious. Was his Mini parked with the engine running, in a remote country lane, a pipe from the exhaust into the car. Was a hot bath and a sharp razor... before the advent of natural gas, a pillow, taps on full, head in the oven.

Flamboyant:

Full of risks.

Jumping from Hungerford Bridge into the Thames... suppose he didn't lose consciousness when he hit the water? Would he have the courage not to swim? Bertram had always been a strong swimmer, won cups at school. Or, in front of an Underground train? Horrible images sprang to mind: Bertram lying between the rails, his legs severed at the thigh, rush hour commuters lining the edge of the platform staring down at him, some fainting as blood gushed from his wounds, Bertram reaching for the live rail, unable to move, fingers stretched, praying that he would not survive. His Mini, again... foot down, swerving into the path of an oncoming truck. Only, somebody else might get injured, killed – he didn't want that.

Signalling Lorenzo for the bill.

While he waited, his favourite fantasy...

The Austrian Tirol. He and Gerry had spent three weeks there, one Spring, touring in Gerry's old 3.4 Jaguar, his 'Morse-mobile', he called it. A little village called Zims, they'd stayed two nights in the only hotel, the Gasthof Thurner, second floor room with a balcony, the river a torrent at that time of the year, the mountains rising above them all around. Bertram picturing a late afternoon meal, some schnapps – they brewed it locally, sold it under the counter in all the bars, quart flagons – walking up into the mountains, a glorious red sunset over the snow, walking as far and as high as he could. Evidently hypothermia was a painless death, you just lay down, went to sleep.

No documentation from which he could be identified.

Probably wouldn't be found for months, anyway. If ever.

Didn't want to give his parents the pleasure of refusing to come to his funeral.

Aware that Lorenzo had placed the bill on his table.

That Celeste was standing behind him.

Heard himself saying, 'Celeste.'

Celeste saying, 'You're supposed to say more than that, Bertram. You're supposed to say, "Celeste, what a pleasant surprise, do sit down. Can I order you anything, a drink, perhaps?"' When Bertram failed to react, Celeste, turning to Lorenzo, saying, 'A large G&T, plenty of ice, and whatever it was he had in that empty glass there.'

Bertram saying, 'This is too much of a coincidence.'

Celeste: 'Of course it is. How many times did you tell us? You and Gerry's anniversary meal... how you still come here every year. How, you couldn't stand visiting his grave, this was the next best thing.'

Celeste pulling out a chair, sitting down.

Bertram saying, 'Not the next best thing. Gerry would have appreciated this gesture far more than my visiting his grave.'

'Sure, and it's a lot more fun.'

Bertram saying, 'I don't like shellfish.'

Celeste saying, 'I'll pass on that one.'

Bertram saying, as Lorenzo arrived with the drinks, 'What are you doing here, Celeste?'

Celeste took a sip of her drink, said, 'I'm going to have to go easy on this stuff, I'm parked on a yellow. I have to take a cab home, the Merc will be towed in the morning. You know how Harry hates unnecessary expense.'

Finished the drink. Called for another.

Bertram, not touching his third grappa, waiting for Celeste to answer his question.

Celeste saying, 'It's Harry…'

'What about Harry?'

'I need to talk to someone before I go nuts.'

Finishing the second gin and tonic.

Looking around for Lorenzo, saying, 'Fuck the Merc.'

Bertram picking up his grappa.

Extending the glass.

Saying to Celeste: '*Salut.*'

D enise wishing it would go away, this feeling that every-thing was so boringly stereotypical. Barbara's beloved Old Rectory, with its stone-paved floors, doors that wouldn't close properly, low timbered ceilings, granite and mortar walls, deep, recessed windows…

It was everything.

Even the evening meal, Mandy tucked upstairs in bed after a quick snack, tired from the long train journey and fast asleep, despite the unfamiliar surroundings. Hand-turned soup bowls, vegetable stew with wild rice and herbs from the garden, home-cultivated yoghurt – God, that tasted awful! Jug of decaf-feinated coffee sitting on the range of the wood-burner, waiting for Barbara or Jack to get up and fetch it over to the table, Barbara finally saying, 'Jack, the coffee.' Denise having to ask if there was any sugar, Barbara saying, 'Sorry, I forgot to put it out. Neither Jack or I use it.'

Use it?

What did that imply?

Jack or I?

Denise, angry with herself that she should feel the need to condone her own actions, saying, 'You know me, I couldn't put on weight, even if I tried.'

Liking the sting in the tail.

Barbara, not missing the inference, saying 'Bitch! I can't help it, stuck at that fucking drawing-board all day…'

Jack: 'All night, too, often as not.'

'…besides, I'm a contented woman, a fat, contented tabby.'

Laughing.

Taking Jack's hand across the table.

Denise thinking, Why am I finding this situation so intolerable?

Barbara and Jack.

As if Barbara had betrayed her.

At the station this afternoon, seeing Barbara, with Jack, waiting for her on the platform, Denise had been excited and then angry, assuming Barbara was attempting to take control of her life, bury her marriage for good, throw Jack in her path, expecting her to seek solace.

Comfort.

God, how she wished she could be like that.

Later, showing her round the orchard, before it got too dark, 'Coxes Orange Pippins, the real thing, shake them and they rattle, not like that crap you buy in the supermarkets…' Taking her to the barn, that year's harvest laid out on straw, saying, 'These will be good to eat right through to the spring, just as long as you chuck out any bruised ones…' Denise thinking of Jack, his tongue, Giles so rarely ever doing that, the only time she had ever felt *that* good, in the kitchen, just a hundred yards away, amusing Mandy, cooking dinner. Barbara saying, 'Of course, you have to watch out. For example, you can't store onions in the same place, the apples will end up tasting of onions.' Denise saying, 'But, you don't grow onions.'

Barbara, 'Yes, but if I did.'

Then: 'Anyway, what fucking time do I have to be growing vegetables?'

Then: 'It's changed my life… Jack.'

Denise feeling incredibly stupid.

Saying, 'You and Jack?'

Barbara, affecting wide-eyed surprise.

'It wasn't obvious?'

Denise, 'Why didn't you tell me? How long…?'

What was that song?

'…Has this been going on?'

Trying to remember the last time Jack had rung her, said he was going to be in London, could they meet up for a drink, lunch?

It hadn't been that long ago.

Barbara flustered.

Denise had never seen Barbara flustered before…

Not about anything.

'It just happened. We just got together for sex, at first, the both of us agreed we were missing a good seeing-to – then, me staying over, Jack staying over, it seemed the obvious move, after a while, Jack moving in.'

Denise saying, again, 'Why didn't you tell me?'

Barbara looking at her, then saying, 'Guilt, I suppose.' Then: 'Though, why the fuck I should feel guilty, I don't know. It was only a one night stand, for fuck's sake.'

Denise saying, 'It's getting a little chilly out here, shall we go in?'

And then the worst moment.

Dinner almost ready.

Barbara, upstairs in her studio, 'I have to make just this one call to the States, fucking art director is an absolute toss-pot. Trouble is, it's me who has to do all the extra work when his ideas don't work out.'

Barbara always happy to remind everybody of the incompetence, the stupidity that made it that much harder for her to produce a decent illustration.

Her favourite… How many times had Denise heard that story? *Jaws*, the book and the film, both, a huge international success. Barbara asked to do the illustration for a book called *Claws*, rabid badger hurtling up through the ground, about to attack a family having a picnic, Barbara explaining to the art director that a badger, rabid or otherwise, didn't have quite the same primordial frisson as a Great White; telling the art director he could fuck off with his commission.

Denise alone with Jack in the kitchen.

Jack, behind her, his hands lightly on her waist, saying, 'This doesn't have to make any difference, Denise, I want you to know that. All you have to do is call.'

Denise saying, 'Oh, sod off, Jack.'

Now, after dinner, Denise saying, 'Perhaps, we could ring the station, check the times of the trains in the morning?'

Barbara saying, 'Christ, Denise, aren't we being a little childish about this. We're all grown-ups, here, you know.'

The dishwasher beginning its cycle.

Denise saying, 'It doesn't feel right. If it doesn't feel right it's not right.

'I feel uncomfortable…
'I feel I'm intruding, making you two uncomfortable…
'I feel I should be with Giles, back in London…'
Barbara saying, 'You do talk a load of old balls, sometimes.'
Leaving the table.
Making the phone call.

Clive Blissett had been in better moods, pissed off that
he'd done nothing better with his evening than drop
three big ones on the baccarat table at Chester's, then,
why did he never learn…? Pulling the peroxide tart who, right
now, had her head buried between his legs, making noises like
a pig at the fucking trough… maybe, he should dump her at
the first service station.

Jimmy, his driver, taking the call in the front, over the intercom, saying, 'Nestor Rodriguez?' Clive telling him to patch it
through, then saying to the tart, 'Take a break, babe, put your
face back on.' Not even having tried to remember her name…
she'd told him, three times at least, back at the casino, but –
what the fuck? – a babe was a babe, end of story. Picking up the
extension, saying, 'Nestor, all my life I knew, I was a good boy,
I'd be taking this call.'

Two-fifteen a.m, London. Had to be around seven in the
evening, local time, Tingo Maria.

The six door Merc, gun metal grey, tinted windows, TV
antennae, Jimmy holding it in the outside lane, despite there
was no traffic to speak of, who knows what the fuck speed he
was doing…

That was Jimmy's business.

The M4, out past the turn-off for Heathrow. To the left, the
landing lights of the big fuckers coming in – you could just
make them out – Clive's place, ten bedroom Victorian farmhouse, just outside Wokingham, this time of night, you were
looking at half an hour.

No more.

Nestor saying, 'We've been throwing a different curve… I
needed to check you're still interested.'

Clear as a bell.

Ten thousand miles away, the whole of the fucking Atlantic Ocean between them.

'Nestor, we're talking dogs and lamp posts.'

'This is what I hoped.'

'Right from the start, didn't I make that clear? You chose to boost your cut, go elsewhere, that's your business.'

'So, we can sit down and talk, right?'

'That depends. You know what they say about monkeys and peanuts... what happened, your monkey fall out of the tree?'

'Clive, do you hear me laughing?'

'Okay, I'll drop the menagerie.'

Nestor saying, 'Harry Street, you two ever do business?'

'It's a small world.'

Then: 'The monkey, right?'

'I'm not getting a good feeling... I'm starting to think, Nestor, is this a man I can trust?'

'Soon as you feel that...'

'We talk the same language.'

Clive thinking, Not on your life, sunshine. Saying, 'Tell me, Nestor, was it a photo-finish?'

'I'm not with you?'

'My bid?'

'It's more complicated.'

'How, more complicated?'

Into darkness.

The next lit section of the motorway when they hit Windsor.

Nestor saying, 'This Harry, we were about to shake hands, he's got the whole picture.'

Clive smiling.

Dipped beams, across the central reservation, heading into town. Hiss of tyres on the road. The tart, through with her make-up kit, helping herself to another drink, vodka tonic, wash the taste of his prick from her mouth.

Clive saying, 'Any contingency, that's a straight fee, over and above anything we work out.'

'Clive...'

'Just so we're clear.'

Nestor saying, 'You get a second chance, here, you want to blow that? Clive, all I'm saying is this – you cover this problem, we get to sit down and talk.'

Clive, knowing he was beat, saying, 'Will you listen to this man? What do you do at Christmas, Nestor, do you sell presents to your family?'

Nestor saying, 'You ain't family.'

Then: 'Here, he would be known as a *sicario*, you have somebody in mind?'

Clive saying, 'I'm a hands-on man.'

Nestor: 'Sometimes, it makes sense to delegate.'

Clive: 'Not if it means missing out on all the fun.'

Thinking, .45 Hydroshock.

The first one in the country.

See how she flies.

Saying to Nestor, 'I'll get back to you.'

Pulling down the vanity tray, over the intercom, telling Jimmy to hold it steady, 'Give me five minutes.' Building two lines of coke, saying to the tart, 'You want some of this, or what?'

The tart saying, 'I don't do drugs.'

Clive saying, 'Fuck this,' then, through to Jimmy, again, saying, 'Pull over. Now.'

The Merc on the hard shoulder, Clive saying to the tart...

'Out!'

Ray not about to take 'no' for an answer.

Not tonight.

Not after the day he'd had today.

First, the funeral – what a bunch of hypocritical shits his family were. None of them ever had a good word to say for his old lady when she was alive, steered clear of her like the plague. There was only the old man, and he'd been brain dead as long as Ray could remember. Would have to be, putting up with her all his married life.

Then the Paddy.

Bold as brass.

You had to hand it to him.

Ray, at first, more than nervous – shit-scared, in fact – this big geezer coming from out of nowhere at his old lady's funeral, knowing more about Ray than the rest of those cunts there put together. Ray not stupid enough to offer any lip, the Paddy looking like he was well up for anything, even at his mother's funeral. Ray wondering – still wondering – why he'd just sat there when Ray did the business on his motor. The Paddy giving him a lift back to the house, not in the Roller, some modern piece of junk. Talking about Ray's bike, turned out he knew a thing or two about motorbikes himself, used to ride them when he was a kid, back in Ireland. Telling Ray how it was going to be all right between them, 'Right up your street,' he said. Ray starting to think this might be his lucky day. The Paddy obviously a bit special…

Different league altogether.

Ray asking if he wanted to come in for a drink.

A sandwich.

The Paddy saying, 'I don't think so.'

His old lady, remembering her, used to say, when he was a kid, before she got ill, 'Every cloud has a silver lining.'

Not for her, it hadn't.

But, Ray, no longer pissed off about the outlay on the CBR, getting the dents knocked out… the respray.

Thinking, bet the Roller cost a fuck sight more.

Now, the old man off to stay with his mum's sister, Aunt Phil, for a few days, over the river, in Wandsworth, she had a two bedroom council flat there, one of those high rises, stairs always stank of piss. Aunt Phil saying to him, after the funeral, 'Ray will be all right, he's hardly a kid, any more. It will do you good, getting away from here for a bit.' Ray thinking, It would have done him more good he'd done it years ago. Aunt Phil promising Ray's old man she would make him his favourite rhubarb crumble, 'It won't be as good as Lou's, but I'll do my best.' Aunt Phil, a widow herself for ten years, Ray thinking, Aye, aye, bit of old hanky-panky going on here, his mother not yet cold in her grave.

Then remembering she had been cremated.

Didn't even exist, any more.

Just dust.

Fucking windy today, too. Who knew where bits of her would fetch up?

Susanne, offended when he said this to her.

'That's not in very good taste, Ray.'

Over for the night, the first time the two of them spending the whole night together. Undressing with the light out, Ray's room at the top of the stairs, couldn't swing a cat… single bed, Airfix models of motorbikes everywhere you looked, blank spaces on the walls where Ray had taken down all the pin-ups before Susanne arrived. Ray getting in first, nearest the wall, Susanne spoiling it all by saying, 'I came on today, so we can't, you know…'

Ray saying, 'Fucking 'ell, now, she tells me.'

Susanne cuddling up to him, Ray not believing how nice it felt, Susanne's body all warm, her boobs squashed up against his chest, her hair down there tickling his thigh, Ray thinking, Christ, she's got more than I have, a right fucking nest.

Susanne saying, 'I'm so sorry about your mum, Ray.'

Ray saying, 'You trying to turn me off, or what?'

Susanne: 'I'm here for you, Ray. I always will be.'

Feeling himself going hard, against her leg.

Susanne saying, 'Is that what you call being turned off?'

Giggling in the dark.

Tongue in his ear.

Taking hold of him between her legs.

Ray putting his hand down there. Susanne intercepting his hand with her own, holding his wrist, saying, 'Ray, I told you, I can't.'

Ray saying, 'Why not? What difference does it make?'

Susanne: 'It's not right, that's all. Besides, I've got something in there.'

'I knew that! Do you think I'm stupid, or something?'

Susanne kissing his chest, then his belly, licking then biting, but not enough that it hurt, saying, 'Shall I do this? Would you like that?' Ray not believing what she was doing, imagining his old lady doing a thing like that to his old man. What if he couldn't help himself, came in her mouth? Saying, 'Susanne, no don't…'

Susanne saying, 'Ray, let me.'

Ray saying, 'Take it out.'

Then: 'You know, what you got in.'

Susanne, her head back beside his on the pillow, kissing him, Ray turning his mouth away thinking, Fuck, she just had that mouth on my prick, do I want to taste my own fucking prick?

Susanne rolling away from him, doing something, then rolling back, saying, '… Ray?' Ray saying, 'Did you do it?'

Susanne saying, 'Ray,' again. Holding herself tight against him, Ray moving his weight on top of her, Susanne opening her legs, helping him, Ray not sure if he was in her or not, Susanne saying, 'Keep still,' guiding him with her hand, making a funny noise, Ray thinking he was hurting her but not giving a fuck. Surprised how wet it was.

Salty.

Cold seawater.

Ray moving.

This, his very first time…

Thinking of summer holidays: crabs, crawling all over each other, dying in his bucket.

Susanne saying, 'Ray! Ray!'

Coming inside her.

Susanne stroking his head.

After a while, saying:

'I'll wash these sheets out for you in the morning.'

Chapter 7
Perhaps She'll Die

Bertram wondered why he had never thought of it before: forget pills, internal combustion engine emissions, hot baths and bleeding, gas ovens, bridges, water, trains, trucks... the ice cold blanket of dusk in the Austrian Tirol...

Aware that he was still pissed.

How much grappa?

Ten-thirty a.m.

The Gaggia making the usual obnoxious noises...

Celeste still asleep in his bed.

The perfect, absolutely fool-proof, money back guaranteed method of committing suicide...

Spend the night with Harry's wife.

Oh, yes, Bertram.

Didn't even have to think about it.

That easy.

Finding two cups, French, octagonal, purple glaze – all in my head – not sure... if Celeste took sugar.

Or milk.

Anything, just so long as it woke her up, got her out of his bed, out of the house. Where the fuck was the car pound when you got towed away in Fulham? Bertram – so, okay, I'm an old fart – had never been in a position where he got towed away. Seldom picked up a ticket, even. Had a resident's permit for the Mini... had to, if you didn't want to park somewhere west of Hounslow every night, catch the underground back in.

Maybe, it's because I'm a Londoner....

Sing, Bertram, sing.

Dreading how he was going to feel when the alcohol wore off. Pouring the cappuccino.

Where the fuck was the cocoa tin?

Would Celeste even notice?

No chocolate top?

Celeste standing in the door of the kitchen...

Saying, 'So, okay, Bertram, win some, lose some.'

Then: 'What the fuck was that racket? I thought you were dying in here?'

So completely unfair.

Spent the night.

Slept together.

Nothing more...

Try telling Harry that.

Just likely to believe that in a million years.

Saying, 'The coffee machine. You want some?'

The two of them staggering back to his place from Lorenzo's, only making it because they each had each other to lean on... introducing Celeste to Noddy, the iguana, Celeste saying, throwing off her coat, searching through the bottles on the living room cabinet, 'Christ, isn't there anything decent I can drink?' Then: 'That is probably the ugliest creature I have ever seen in my life! What is the point of keeping an animal like that?'

Bertram, not bothering to explain.

Apologising for having no gin, 'I never touch the stuff.'

Celeste saying, 'Vodka, yuck! Always has that burnt taste.'

Finding her a glass of Spanish brandy...

Then – just how the fuck were you supposed to entertain a woman? – showing her his collection of plastic shopping bags... his pride and joy. Big metal filing cabinet he'd bought at some car boot sale, each bag in its own hanging folder. Telling Celeste how, every time he left the house, more important than the right jacket, the right shoes... he'd go to that cabinet, pick out the right bag for the right occasion. Weird things – don't ask him why – like, if he was going to Sainsbury's, he'd take a Waitrose bag, and vice versa...

His favourite, for every day use, a little Dillon's Bookshop bag, quarter size, hung from his wrist, just large enough to carry his loose change, reading glasses, Filofax, and Paracetamol, just in case one of his heads came on when he was out. Showing her the prize of his collection, a Biba bag, circa '65, not from the big store in Kensington High Street that went bust – from the original store in Church Street, remembering how his old man always used to go on about how there were no curtains on the changing cubicles, picturing all those hippies in their Lionel's and tie-dyes, standing there with a hard on, saying, not even looking at the new Laura Ashley was going to cost them half a week's wages, 'Yeah, that's really nice, that really suits you.' Bertram, in his office above Regent Street, seeing the same thing, day in, day out, across the road…

Apart from the hard on.

What changes?

Bertram, now taking the packet of Beecham's Powders from the cabinet above the sink, pulling out and unfolding one of the papers, pouring the powder into a glass of water.

Stirring it with his finger.

Before drinking.

Celeste, behind him, saying, 'Don't offer me anything to eat, I might throw up.'

Last night, taking one of the plastic bags from his file, nothing special to anyone else, a Continental Airlines Duty Free bag, from when he went to Los Angeles with Gerry, Gerry had a one liner in a co-financed production, the director insisting, fuck the cost, it had to be the real thing, I want some guy used to lowering the drawbridge, he takes his dog for a walk in the morning – Gerry swore it was no word of a lie, his one line, 'Your horse is saddled, sir…' Bertram along for the trip, disappointed everything out there came in brown paper sacks…

Celeste putting the bag over her head, saying, 'What is it turns you on, Bertram? Tell me, I'd really like to know.' Bertram saying, 'Celeste, you are seriously wasting your time,' Celeste not willing to take 'no' for an answer.

Saying, 'You can fantasise, I won't mind.'

And: 'What did you and Gerry used to do? Short of buggering you, what could he do that I can't?'

Bertram saying, 'This is so embarrassing.'

Celeste saying, 'No, really…'

Bertram, holding her tight, saying, 'Celeste, it's to do with desire – it's to do with love.' Then, when she was through crying, Celeste saying, 'Bertram, tell me about Tim.'

'Tim is history.'

Celeste saying, 'If Tim is history, how come Harry is always talking about him in his sleep?'

Bertram saying, 'You wouldn't want to know… Harry wouldn't even want to know.'

Then, in bed, Celeste, tight up close to him, saying, 'Suppose Harry did know?'

Now, Celeste searching through her bag for her car keys, saying, 'It's still there, will be a miracle.'

Bertram: 'If it's not, come back. I'll call a cab for you.'

Then: 'You sure you won't have any coffee?'

'Uh huh.'

Meaning no.

Bertram saying, 'One small favour, Celeste.'

Celeste saying, 'Don't look so worried… I'm not going to breath a word.'

Bertram saying, before he could think about it, change his mind, 'No…

'I'd sooner you did.'

G iles, not sure why he had agreed to meet Jane again today.

Three o'clock at the house.

And Chris, for a drink, lunchtime?

Had he gone fucking mad?

A complete fucking masochist?

Working on a filler that had now become an urgent deadline – didn't they all? – 'Thanksgiving in the USA', research, as much as he needed, complete for weeks, all he had to do was write the fucking thing. Nice angle, spiralling poverty in the USA, Graeme, not sure a London readership would give a fuck, giving the go ahead just so long as they made the date…

'Cold Turkey.'

Christ, was Graeme ever a difficult bastard to please?

Then Chris ringing…

Just as he was getting stuck in.

Saying: 'How about lunch? My shout.'

Giles saying, 'So, okay, Simon Mates was very funny.'

'Not if you were in his shoes.'

Then, 'I have some good news. How about The White Tower?'

'You know I hate Indian.'

'The best in town?'

'And the most expensive.'

'What the fuck, if I'm paying?'

Then: 'What about fish, then? Sheeky's? You remember…'

Giles laughing.

Couldn't help it.

Chris as incorrigible as ever…

Saying, 'The live tadpole in the salad, came with the poached turbot hollandaise?'

'Sure we'd get a free lunch out of it.'

'No such thing as a free lunch.'

'Tell me about it.'

'The waiter saying, "Shows it's fresh, sir."'

Both of them laughing.

Then, Giles: 'Game, set, and match.'

Chris saying, 'I don't suppose you've heard about Helen Monkton?'

'What about her?'

'Up for my old job.'

Giles saying, 'You're joking!'

Then: 'Oh, fuck off.'

Chris saying, 'Why don't we just make it a drink… Flaubert's?'

Where else?

Cold cuts, cheese, and, Chris, now across the table from him – how come Chris was always such a good idea at a distance – saying, 'A rather nice South African Cabinet Savignon, fuck the politics, fuck the Australians, we're talking Old Country, here.'

Giles saying, 'I don't know.'

Chris saying, 'You really think some white *nouveau* middle class embargo, on a country so far removed, the water goes down the plug-hole the other way, is going to make any difference?'

'It's a gesture.'

'For fuck's sake, grow up, Giles.'

Then: 'Anyway, it will be all over soon, the natives are restless. Fuck Nelson Mandela… here's to Idi Amin, a man not afraid to show his true colour.'

Then: 'I've been offered a job…'

'Chris, I'm so pleased.'

'Three guesses.'

'*Venue*?'

'In one, you bastard. Same fucking pay as the mail boy, but, what the fuck, a job is a job.'

'You? Working for a co-operative?'

Chris ordering the South African wine.

Same New Zealand waitress.

With the blonde hair.

Chris, saying to her, 'I'd have thought you'd be in somewhere like Patagonia by now. Tips not what you thought... Mean bastards, the British.'

Giles saying, 'Tell me about the job.'

'General Editor. Less pay, more poke... I'd just love to see Graeme's face when he hears.'

'Why? Do you think he'll be upset?'

'You are joking? You don't really think he wanted to lose me, do you? His hands were tied. Just how long go you think Helen the Monkfish would have hung around for – her Graeme dropped off the social register. No more invites to Mustique, big, gaping hole in his diary on The Glorious Twelfth?'

'I don't think Graeme would want to wish you any harm.'

'He will once he checks the comparative circulation figures over the next few months. Will take a while, but just remember, you heard it here first.'

'You never were short on self-confidence, were you, Chris?'

'Why, the fuck, should I be?'

Giles, for the first time, making a connection.

Chris and Barbara...

How similar they were.

Giles saying to Denise, once...

Once? A lot more than once.

'You can't see yourself, Denise... the way you fawn over that fucking woman, one word from her, you turn into a simpering idiot. What is it about her, she's so great...? A failed artist, hack illustrator with a big mouth.'

Then, making the other connection.

Oh Christ! Was he like that with Chris?

Thinking of Denise, in Wales, now. Barbara wouldn't waste any time setting her up with that fucking teepee dweller, meddling cow that she was.

Checking his watch, two-fifteen.

Oh, fuck, Jane...

An afternoon of 'Itsy-witsy'.

Mr Biggy-Wiggy.

She should be so lucky.

The waitress arriving at their table with the South African Savignon.

Chris making a big deal out of sniffing the cork, nodding for the waitress to pour some wine, lifting the glass to the light, checking the viscosity by twirling the glass, bringing it to his nose, savouring the bouquet…

Taking for ever.

Everybody at the surrounding tables – Chris, now, with their full attention – thinking: What a prat!

Giles thinking, Oh Christ, he's not going to pull that one again, is he?

Knowing what would happen next.

Chris taking a sip, running the wine around his tongue, the roof of his mouth, swallowing, grasping his throat, screaming, falling off his chair, on his back on the floor, legs kicking, arms thrashing.

Everybody laughing.

Clapping.

Even the New Zealand waitress.

Chris saying to her, 'See, knew I'd win you over in the end.'

Giles remembering telling Denise about Chris's party piece, after the first time he had seen him do it, taken by surprise, just like everybody else…

Denise saying, 'Is he never going to grow up?'

Absolute disdain in her voice.

Humourless bitch.

Saying to Chris, 'This will have to be it, I've got a lot on this afternoon.'

Thinking of Jane.

Knickers in a twist.

Camped out on his doorstep.

Chris saying, 'I wouldn't worry about that. You can tell Graeme Tate to fuck off any time you like… come and work with me, on *Venue*.'

Giles laughing.

Saying: 'And on the same salary as you.'

Chris saying, 'Christ, I hadn't thought of that! No justice in this fucking world, is there.'

'Oh, I don't know so much.'

Chris saying, 'Don't start all that old bollocks again.'

Both of them laughing.

Then Chris saying, 'You're in such a mad tearing rush... how about we see if that Kiwi tart has any of her *Rimmy* left?'

Giles thinking.

There was something about Chris.

You just had to laugh.

Then:

'Rimmy'.

Wondering if Jane would be up for that.

Ray, still with a big fat Cheshire cat grin on his face, couldn't help it, hidden beneath the scarf, the tinted visor of his helmet. Across to Putney, picking up the bike, nice job, too – good as new, despite they took twice as long as they said they would – then, powering back over Hammersmith Bridge, heading straight from the repair shop to Chiswick, get sorted this job the Paddy wanted doing for him, spotted the two Japanese tourists on the bridge, taking photos of each other, the river behind them.

Couldn't believe his luck.

What with the rest of it...

House to himself.

Susanne last night – despite the fucking mess, thought he was bleeding to death when he clocked the sheets, up for his first pee, just when it got light, Susanne saying, 'You just go and have a good wash. I'll sort this out.'

Then cooking him breakfast.

Luxuries will never cease!

Big fry up.

Before she fucked off to work...

Now this.

Pulling over.

Saying, 'Clickety-click? Two... both?'

Holding an invisible camera to his face, waggling his finger up and down, like he was pressing a button.

The man coming across to the bike, the woman smiling.

The man saying, 'Thank you, thank you.'

Putting all the weight on the you.

Like you would if you were saying, 'Fuck you'.

Handing Ray the camera and going back to stand with his wife.

Saying to Ray, his arm round his wife, now, the two of them leaning against the bridge, 'Just to press, it does all things.'

Whacking the CBR into gear, driving off, the Pentax zipped up inside his leather jacket.

Didn't look back, once.

Chink bastards!

Hadn't felt this good since the day he passed his test, got rid of the 'L' plates, expected every other fucker on the road to notice...

Flooring the exhaust, left, after the bridge, on to the Great West Road, left again at Sutton Court Road, just before Chiswick Flyover and the start of the M4, going through what the Paddy had told him...

The fifteen-pounder tucked in the pannier.

The Paddy saying, 'Piece of piss, Ray. You could do it standing on your head.'

And: 'No "buts" about it... you get carried away on this.'

Writing down the names in a notebook, tearing out the sheet, passing it to Ray, 'This is important... she has to know you know her name... and you have to mention...'

Celeste.

Ray, talking to himself as he hit Chiswick High Road, the snarl up of traffic around Sainsbury's...

'Denise.'

'Celeste.'

'Celeste.'

'Denise.'

Hoping he wasn't going to fuck it up.

Get them the wrong way round.

The Paddy saying, 'You get this right, there's a one-er in it for you. Plus, we forget the other business.'

Ray, couldn't help himself, saying, 'Fuck you, or what? I could have been dead.'

Then: 'You had it coming.'

The Paddy saying, 'Don't push it, son.'

Ray, under the railway bridge, turning left again, pulling into the curb, checking what the Paddy had written down for him, the name of the street, Ray admitting to himself he never had been much good remembering names...

Well, fuck you.

In one.

Clocking the numbers.

Had to be a bit down.

On the right.

Still grinning.

Susanne, cooking dinner tonight.

None of his old man's shit.

The Paddy, probably right for the first time in his life…

Putting the Pentax in the pannier.

Taking out the hammer…

Piece of piss.

B ack indoors by two-thirty.
Denise looking at the bed – Mandy, protestations ignored, pushed into a hot bath – thinking, How long…? Twenty-four hours? I don't believe this, I really don't.

Wanting to walk straight back out of the house.

But, where?

Hating herself for putting her nose to the pillows.

Recognising the perfume, but where?

Finding a hair.

Then a short hair.

Different colours.

Sitting on the edge of the bed, her bed, Giles's bed, weeping…

Thinking: 'You shit!'

Hearing the front door bell ring.

Then again.

Mandy, from the bathroom, calling, 'Door, mummy!'

Whoever it was…

Not having much patience.

Harry liked to tell this story about The Mozambique, despite he owned the place, swore it was no word of a lie. Young dip-shit, stud in his nose, pony-tail, Miriam behind the bar, him bending her ear all night, how he was into this, how he was into that, entertaining visions of how he just might be in with a chance…

Get inside her pants.

Before the night was out.

Harry breaking into his own story, laughing, saying, 'Fat chance, you knew Miriam.'

Turned out, this punter was a photographer, mail order catalogues… skirt, somebody's niece from Argos, you wouldn't give it the time of day, posed in front of a curtain rail for a shower unit, stretched out on one of those mattresses supposed to do wonders for a bad back…

You had a back problem.

Bird like that.

That was your fucking look out.

Harry telling Ross…

How many times had Ross heard this story?

'Apocryphal,' Mary had said, when he told her.

Ross saying, 'What the fuck does that mean?'

Apologising for swearing in front of Mary.

Mary, 'And so you should,' then saying, 'It's a tall story, Ross, gets better with the telling.'

Not with Harry, it didn't. Perched on a bar stool. Usual lunchtime crowd.

Ross the only one in the place drinking coffee.

Harry, in his stride by now…

'Miriam had his bar bill, had to present it in evidence… nine margaritas, three-fifty a throw. This fuckhead staggers round to his motor in Berwick Street, key won't fit in the lock, you know how it goes – Mr Plod standing there, the tit-wit blowing into his bag, the tit-wit thinking, This will be one to tell the boys, saying, "Fair cop, Officer," and guess what?'

Ross saying, 'Under the limit.'

Harry: 'Too fucking right…

'then what happens?'

'The fucker sues.'

Harry, 'And do you know what?'

Ross saying, 'He wins.'

Harry saying, 'You heard this story before, right?'

'Right.'

Harry saying, 'So, tell me why we need to speak.'

Harry had a theory.

Just so long as you needed somebody, needed a piece of his action, every time, just tell him what he wanted to hear.

Make it up as you went along.

What the fuck.

Ross calling him, saying, 'I need to talk,' that was warning bells.

Ross arriving at The Mozambique with a face like a wet week…

That was:

Well, okay.

Ten years is a long time.

Maybe, too long.

Ross, on the wagon for fifteen years, Harry offering him a drink. Ross saying, 'Coffee will do.' Harry saying, 'You know, we ought to talk more often,' thinking, Talk? Why should I want to talk to the fucking chauffeur?

Telling him the story.

Thinking, Weights and Measures? Didn't he pay enough to have that covered?

Thinking about Celeste…

Rolling in at ten-thirty this morning.

Harry saying, 'Where the fuck you been?'

Celeste, not saying, screaming, 'Good fucking question, Harry. All my life, where the fuck have I been?'

Harry thinking, What the hell…?

A drunk is a drunk.

Waiting for Ross to get to the point.

When he'd finished his third scotch, Ross on his second coffee, saying, 'You got something to say, say it.' Ross shifting around on his bar stool like a big kid, Miriam gone to the other end of the bar, seen Harry in this kind of mood often enough,

Harry saying, 'For fuck's sake, Ross, you got worms, try boiled eggs and a hammer.'

Why should he make it easy?

Ross saying, 'Harry… there's some things I'm not happy about.'

Harry saying, 'Happy…?

'Don't make me laugh.'

R ay, on the doorstep, saying, 'No, not Pizza Express.'
Pleased with his own joke.

The woman, small, fragile – the bird that fell out of the nest in the school playground, all the kids making a circle, not knowing what to do. The teacher, biology teacher – would you believe it? – called down from the teacher's common room, taking one look, grinding the bird under his heel, saying, 'It's for the best.'

Ray…

All the rest of them.

Still in a circle.

Looking at the pool of bits.

New term.

Frost on the ground.

Blood and feathers.

Not squawking any more.

Couldn't imagine it ever had.

Splat! There on the asphalt. Like a gob…

Years later, his old lady throwing up the same kind of shit, missed the toilet bowl, too sick to notice, Ray thinking, Fuck this, I'm just a kid, do I need this?

Then bringing her a cup of tea in bed, saying, 'It's got two sugars…' Never could remember.

His old lady saying, 'You're a good boy, Ray.'

The woman saying, 'What?'

Showing her the hammer.

Ray pushing through the door, trying to remember every word the Paddy had told him, pushing her in front of him, back into the kitchen, the woman saying, like he'd said when his old lady first got ill, 'Do I need this, do I really need this?'

Round the other side of the table... from upstairs, a kid shouting, 'Mummy! It's getting cold.' The woman, surprising Ray, shouting back, 'I'11 be up in a minute.'

Through the tinted visor.

Saying, 'Denise?'

The woman, the kitchen table still between them, saying, 'You can fuck right off!'

Ray, in that other world, divorced from reality, his crash helmet a cushion...

More than physical.

Moon-walking.

Aware of another woman.

Coming down the passage, the front door wide open, her mouth moving.

The first woman screaming, 'Jane!'

Ray running out of the house.

Who needed this shit...

Everything going so good?

Τhe NCP car park, between Wardour Street and Dean Street, Harry rented a permanent bay, the Roller on the second floor, next to the lift. Ross thinking, I could talk till the cows come home, it would make fuck all difference. Harry in front, taking the ramp like he was still a kid, looking back over his shoulder, saying, 'You disappoint me, Ross, you really do.' Ross knowing he could never explain it, how he felt, not being able to look Mary in the eye any more, Mary saying, 'There's something wrong, Ross, I know it... are you seeing somebody else?' Mary, the only woman in his life, having to ask him a question like that, Ross not able to give her a straight answer.

Harry standing there while Ross opened the back passenger door, saying, 'This business with the kid, nothing OTT, right?'

Half in, half out, of the Roller, sitting down, one foot still on the concrete.

Ross trying to place the bloke coming towards them between the rows of parked cars...

Recognising the face.

Not able to put a name.

Harry seeing him, saying, 'Clive – small world.'

Clive leaning into the car, the two of them shaking hands, Clive saying, 'Isn't it just? Thought I recognised the motor.'

Ross remembering him from a riverboat party, few months back, Ross stuck on the boat six hours sipping mineral water, how the fuck could you leave early, stuck on a boat? Harry introducing them, saying, 'Meet the competition.'

Clive, laughing, saying, 'Not me, Harry, I know my limitations.' Ross thinking, Pull the other one you smooth talking fucker...

Clive saying now, 'Been meaning to give you a bell. Heard you'd been having a few problems with the greasers.'

Harry: 'Not that I know of.'

Ross seeing the Nine come out from under Clive's jacket.

Not recognising the model.

Clive saying, 'Shows how much you know, Harry.'

Harry in the back seat of the Roller, Ross still holding the door...

It was like a splatter of red bird shit had appeared on Harry's forehead.

Deafening roar.

Could have heard it all the way to Piccadilly Circus.

Ross noticing:

No recoil to speak of...

Harry saying, 'Oh.'

Just remembered something important.

The interior of the Roller, behind Harry, a right fucking mess.

Ross letting go of the door, backing off a pace, arms extended, palms out, saying, 'I'm out of this... just the hired help, right?'

Clive saying, 'Sure, you are, Ross.'

Ross, not sure if he was swearing or praying.

Jesus Christ, Mother of...

Topping the rise, Dingle Bay in the early morning, the heat of the sun bouncing back from the long grass either side of the road, the sea below a bed of diamonds.

Not making it to 'Mary'.

It was two weeks later when Celeste rang Giles on his home number, late Saturday morning.

She'd been up since eight o'clock, showered and dressed, so far, not touched a drop, going from room to room, then from room to room again, every so often, saying to herself, 'Harry, you big dope.' Saving her tears – not sure what for – maybe the funeral.

If the police ever released the fucking body.

Hearing Giles's voice.

Giles saying, 'Celeste.'

As if he knew she would ring.

'I was afraid your wife might answer.'

'She's got a friend come up to town for the day… Christmas shopping. They're having lunch.'

'Girl-friend?'

'No, a man. Said she'd decided it was her turn to be the other woman.'

'She should watch out – it's not an easy habit to break.'

Then: 'Come over.'

Giles saying, 'Celeste, I read the papers… I'm sorry.'

'Now.'

And: 'Just don't think about it.'

Giles saying, 'It wouldn't be appropriate.'

'Appropriate? What the fuck *is* appropriate?'

'Besides, I've got Mandy.'

'Mandy?'

'My daughter.'

Celeste saying, 'What the fuck? Bring her, too.'

BLOODLINES the cutting-edge crime and mystery imprint...

Smalltime
by Jerry Raine

Smalltime is a taut, psychological crime thriller, set among the seedy world of petty criminals and no-hopers. In this remarkable début, Jerry Raine shows just how easily curiosity can turn into fear amid the horrors, despair and despondency of life lived a little too near the edge.

"Jerry Raine's *Smalltime* carries the authentic whiff of sleazy nineties Britain. He vividly captures the world of stunted ambitions and their evil consequences."— Simon Brett

ISBN 1 899344 13 6 — £5.99

Fresh Blood
edited by Mike Ripley & Maxim Jakubowski

"Move over Agatha Christie and tell Sherlock the News!" This landmark anthology features the cream of the British New Wave of crime writers: John Harvey, Mark Timlin, Chaz Brenchley, Russell James, Stella Duffy, Ian Rankin, Nicholas Blincoe, Joe Canzius, Denise Danks, John B Spencer, Graeme Gordon, the two editors, and a previously unpublished extract from the late Derek Raymond. Includes an introduction from each author explaining their views on crime fiction in the '90s and a comprehensive foreword on the genre from Angel-creator, Mike Ripley.

ISBN 1 899344 03 9 — £6.99

Quake City
by John B Spencer

The third novel to feature Charley Case, the hard-boiled investigator of the future. But of a future that follows the 'Big One of Ninety-Seven' – the quake that literally rips California apart and makes LA an Island.

"Classic Chandleresque private eye tale, jazzed up by being set in the future… but some things never change – PI Charley Case still has trouble with women and a trusty bottle of bourbon is always at hand. An entertaining addition to the private eye canon."

— John Williams, *Mail on Sunday*

ISBN 1 899344 02 0 — £5.99

Outstanding Paperback Originals from The Do-Not Press:

Will You Hold Me?
by Christopher Kenworthy
Christopher Kenworthy's intense, mood-laden stories expertly explore the vulnerable under-belly of human emotion. From the sleazy backstreets of Paris to huddled London bedrooms, his characters inhabit a world where hope too often turns to despair and where compassion is rewarded with malice.

Christopher Kenworthy is a writer at the cutting edge of contemporary fiction, and this is the first collection of his brilliantly original stories.

"The voice is original, plain, pained. The content borders on the gothic. The effect is to reveal both magic and menace as being present in the ordinary." — Geoff Ryman, author of *Was*

ISBN 1 899344 11 X — £6.99

The Users
by Brian Case
The welcome return of Brian Case's brilliantly original '60s cult classic.

"A remarkable debut" —Anthony Burgess

"Why Case's spiky first novel from 1968 should have languished for nearly thirty years without a reprint must be one of the enigmas of modern publishing. Mercilessly funny and swaggeringly self-conscious, it could almost be a template for an early Martin Amis." — *Sunday Times*

ISBN 1 899344 05 5— £5.99

Life In The World Of Women
a collection of vile, dangerous and loving stories by Maxim Jakubowski
Maxim Jakubowski's dangerous and erotic stories of war between the sexes are collected here for the first time, including three major new pieces. Taking in aspects of crime noir, erotica, romance and gritty social drama, *Life In The World Of Women* confirms Maxim Jakubowski as one of Britain's finest and hardest-hitting writers.

"Whatever else it might be – romantic pornography or pornographic romance – *Life* is a bold experiment in self-mythologising fiction." — Nicholas Royle, *Time Out*

"Demonstrates that erotic fiction can be amusing, touching, spooky and even (at least occasionally) elegant. Erotic fiction seems to be Jakubowski's true metier. These stories have the hard sexy edge of Henry Miller and the redeeming grief of Jack Kerouac. A first class collection." — Ed Gorman, *Mystery Scene* (USA)

ISBN 1 899344 06 3 — £6.99

Outstanding Paperback Originals from The Do-Not Press:

A Two Hander
collected poetry by Sara Kestelman & Susan Penhaligon
A new and impressive collection of poetry from two of Britain's most celebrated actresses. Although their careers have sometimes taken different paths, Sara Kestelman and Susan Penhaligon have come together to write poetry touching on every aspect of their separate lives as women, lovers and actresses. The result is a refreshing mix of styles and subjects, with each writer complementing the other perfectly.
1-899-344-08-X £6.99

Funny Talk
edited by Jim Driver
A unique, informative and hilarious collection of new writing on – and around – the theme of comedy. Among the 25 authors: **Michael Palin** on Sid, the Python's driver, **Jeremy Hardy**, **Mark Lamarr**, **Max Bygraves** on his first car, **Mark Steel, Hattie Hayridge, Malcolm Hardee, Norman Lovett, Jon Ronson, Bob Mills**, plus all you ever need to know about good and terrible sit-coms, and 12 new cartoons from **Ray Lowry**. "Thoroughly excellent! " – *Time Out*
ISBN 1 899344 01 2 — £6.95

Deep & Meaningless
The complete JOHN OTWAY lyrics, compiled by John Haxby
The only complete collection of lyrics from the much-loved rock humorist, songwriter and best-selling author. Includes the hits *Really Free* and *Beware of the Flowers*, as well as rare pictures and sleeve shots.
1-899-344-07-1 £5.99

Passport to the Pub
The Tourist's Guide to Pub Etiquette by Kate Fox
(in association with the Brewers & Licensed Retailers Society)
Basic advice and information tourists (and others!) need in order to unravel the mysteries of Britain's pubs. Includes basic rules, do's and don'ts, warnings and tips. Very funny and surprisingly useful for anyone who ever has need to enter a British pub.
1-899-344-09-8 £3.99

All books published by The Do-Not Press are available at local bookshops or by post (post-free in UK, Ireland and other EC countries) from:
The Do-Not Press
PO Box 4215
London
SE23 2QD
Please allow twenty days for delivery and make cheques payable to:
"The Do-Not Press"

The Do-Not Press
Fiercely Independent Publishing

Keep in touch with what's happening at the cutting edge of independent British publishing.

Join The Do-Not Press Information Service and receive advance information of all our new titles, as well as news of events and launches in your area, and the occasional free gift and special offer.

Simply send your name and address to:
The Do-Not Press (Dept. PSD)
PO Box 4215
London
SE23 2QD

There is no obligation to purchase and no salesman will call.

John B Spencer

was born in west London, where he still lives, with his wife Lou, and the youngest of their three sons. He is also a much-respected musician, producer and songwriter and has a number of CDs on the market. This is his fifth novel.